Key Evidence

By the same author

Fifteen Elizabeth Avenue
Run Boy. Run!
A Tragic Accident
Sky High Revenge
A Stroke of Bad Luck
For details go to ghbooks.uk

Key Evidence

Paul J Knight

Gyffarde House Books

ACKNOWLEDGEMENTS

I am grateful to my dear wife, Annette, for her patience and encouragement. I would like to acknowledge and thank my friends, Susan Lawson, Susan Muscroft, for their careful reading; Peter Murphy KC for his professional advice; and the author Liz Shakespeare, for her encouragement. Also thanks to my son, Christopher, for the original cover design which has been adapted for this book.

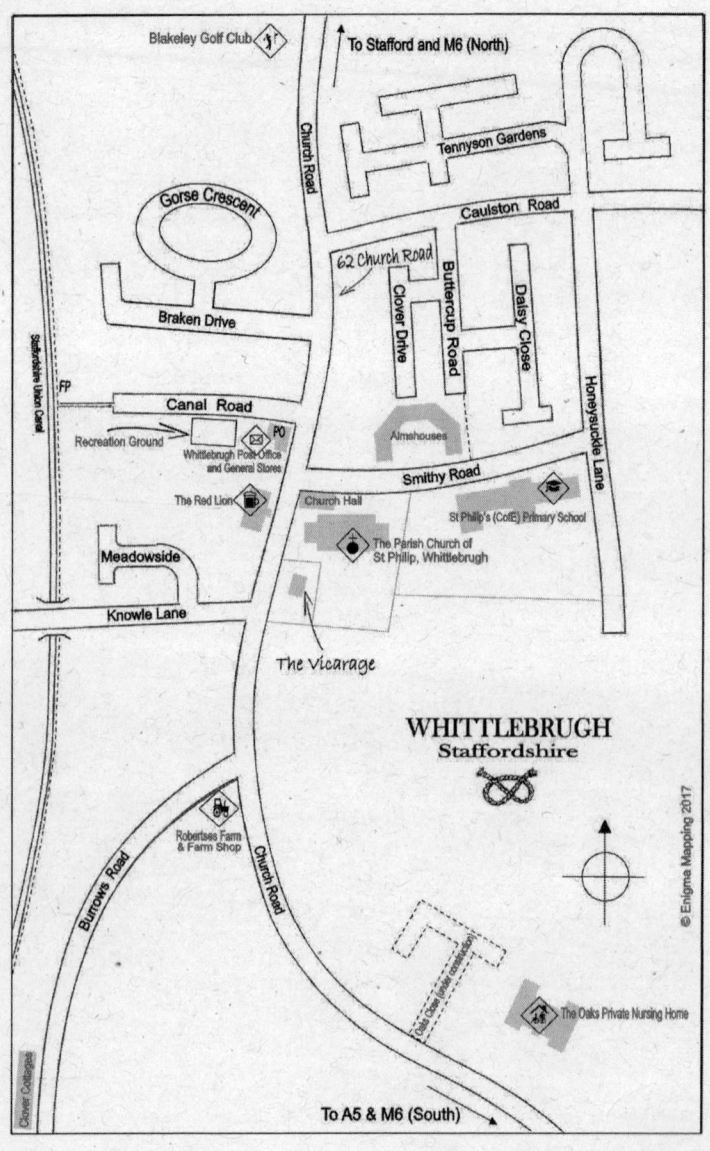

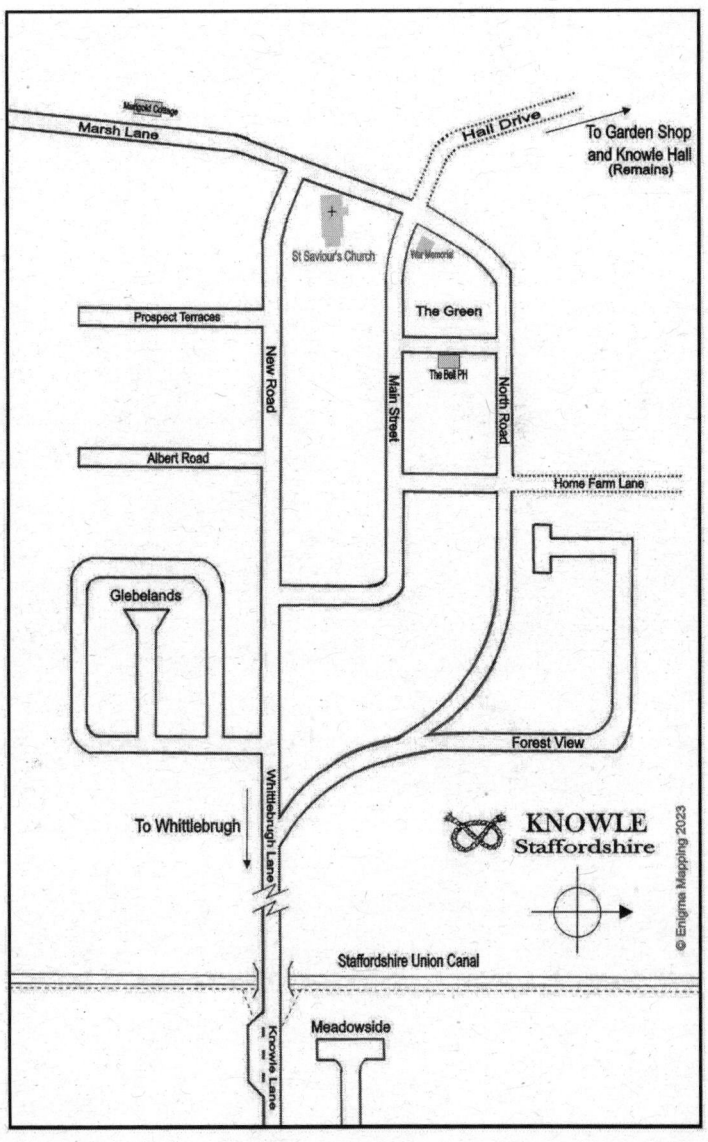

Saturday 5th May

1

In the 1940s, Knowle Hall had burnt down. An electric fire had been left on overnight near a window. The wind blew a curtain onto the hot, unguarded elements. The curtains caught fire and it was soon an inferno. That, at least, was what the fire investigators had concluded. The Hall was gutted and the Greysons decided to abandon it for their London home. The Greyson family had been resident in the Staffordshire village of Knowle since the 17th century and the village lost the benefactor's presence in the community.

The remains of the Hall had been fenced off soon after the fire, though locals could recount childhood adventures into the grounds and amongst the rubble. Over the subsequent years, observant locals could identify masonry and bricks salvaged from the ruins and used as features in the gardens of many of the Knowle village cottages and houses.

One area that was still in use, was the walled garden. The head gardener, as was, continued to grow vegetables and flowers. This had turned into a small business. His son, and his daughter-in-law, Richard and Caroline, had continued after Richard's father and mother had passed away. They had utilised the stable block as storage for materials and equipment. The original greenhouses had been maintained and from these they had been able to provide early crops. They were able to sell these at a premium. Perhaps most sought after were the pineapples from the original pinery, the taste of which was reputed to be 'out of this world'.

One sunny Saturday in early May, Simon and Sharon Curtis drove to Knowle to see what freshly-grown, organic vegetables they could buy from the little shop – a wooden shed adjacent to the Gardener's Cottage. Caroline, hurried over from the cottage as soon as she heard the bell ring. Sharon had already picked up a bunch of carrots and a cauliflower.

'Hello Vicar,' said Caroline brightly. 'Nice to see you again.'

'Good to be back. I just love to use your vegetables for our Sunday dinner. It makes it so special.'

Simon, coughed politely. Sharon glanced at him before continuing. 'I have to admit, though, that it's Simon who does most of the cooking on Sundays as I find myself quite busy in one way or another, if you know what I mean.'

'How long is it since you became our Vicar? It must be what, three years?'

'Just coming up to four.'

'Wow. So David must have left about five years ago.'

'I believe it was soon after his wife went missing in

the January, so about four and a half years. Did you know them well?'

'Quite well. David and Rebecca were a lovely couple. She was vibrant and amiable. They came with such enthusiasm - made everyone feel so welcome,' then added quickly, 'as you and Simon do.'

Simon, who was looking at buckets of cut flowers at the other end of the shed, chuckled.

'I've only picked up little snippets of information about my predecessor. He was clearly very popular.'

'He was. *His* predecessor was, quite frankly, a bit of a bore. Mind you he was getting on a bit. He was a bachelor who was a bit of a bookworm from all accounts. I remember him coming into school in his cassock. Let me tell you we found him a bit scary. Father Downley. Even as a teenager I'd avoid him if I could.'

'So Reverend David must have been a bit of a turnaround.'

'He was, until Rebecca went missing. He changed overnight.'

'So I heard.'

'He became withdrawn. He was only seen occasionally. It didn't help that rumors quickly spread that he had murdered Rebecca and disposed of her body somewhere. Most of us knew that couldn't be true. The police investigated and were unable to find any evidence - well they wouldn't would they? The Bishop gave him compassionate leave and then he left. He was given another job somewhere. I've heard he eventually took a parish somewhere in Yorkshire.'

'Yes, that's what I heard. It sounds so dreadful. I'm not sure if anyone could ever recover from a thing like. Poor man.'

Simon sidled up to her, adding a bunch of flowers into the overflowing shopping basket. 'I think we probably ought to be getting on now, darling.'

'Yes of course.'

Caroline added up the total and Simon paid in cash from his wallet.

'Thank you,' called Caroline as they went through the doorway. 'See you again soon.'

They climbed back into their car and Simon began driving the short journey home to Whittlebrugh. The road took them past St Saviour's Church and through the village, along Whittlebrugh Lane until it became Knowle Lane leading into Whittlebrugh.

'I suppose,' reflected Sharon, 'I should know more about the Staintons. Bishop Stephen told me I would have to pick up the pieces of the tragedy and its aftermath.'

'True, but I think you needed to push ahead with building the churches up again. Frankly, you've had little time for your feet to touch the ground with the three churches and a church school to look after.' The car bumped over the canal bridge.

'True,' agreed Sharon. 'You are wonderful, you know. I couldn't have done this without you.'

'Very true.'

Simon halted at the junction, with Church Road to

the left and Briars Lane to the right, and turned left for the hundred yards or so to the Whittlebrugh Vicarage driveway. 'Anything else on the agenda today?'

'Only the small matter of a sermon. I'll try and finish quickly so we can go out for a quiet drink later. Okay?'

'Suits me.'

-o0o-

Cliff and Tony spent the morning on their new hobby: magnet fishing. Cliff had ordered the necessary equipment from Amazon and it had arrived on Wednesday evening. He called Tony straight away to tell him the good news and they had arranged to meet up at nine on Saturday morning to give-it-a-go. The obvious place to start was the canal. It ran north to south on the western side of Whittlebrugh, passing under the road bridge between Whittlebrugh and Knowle. Cliff arrived first and parked in the layby near the bridge, leaving enough room for Tony to park behind him. It wasn't long before they were standing together unpacking the new 'toy' and discarding the instructions.

After two hours they had become downhearted. Cliff was unreasonably peeved by the interruptions caused by walkers and cyclists on the towpath, and boats passing along the waterway. The only object they had recovered from the mud of the canal was an old spanner – imperial measurement of three-quarters of an inch.

'Well what did you expect,' ribbed Tony, 'treasure on the first drop?'

'But magnet fishers do find valuables. Did you see

that piece about the guys who dredged up a safe from a river in Lincolnshire?'

'I bet, if we were ever to find a safe there would be nothing of value in it – just soggy papers.'

Cliff laughed out loud. 'Laundered money.'

'Very funny!'

Cliff threw the magnet into the canal once more, hitting the surface of the water with a 'plop'. They watched it sink below the surface before he started to pull it back in. He felt resistance. He looked at Tony with a broad grin. 'We're in luck,' he said excitedly. Tony, who was several inches taller, grabbed hold of the rope from behind, and they pulled together. Slowly the item was dragged closer until it broke the surface. 'No, no, no,' wailed Cliff. 'Just a rotten old child's bike.'

'Tough luck! Maybe next time. Shall we throw it back in?'

'Better not. I'll take it to the scrappie. That way we can say we're helping to keep the canal free of rubbish.'

'You carry on if you want. I'm off home.'

'Okay, Tony. I'll catch up with you later. Bye.'

2

Greg and Sally walked into The Red Lion just after seven o'clock. Greg hadn't long been home from his work at Stafford Museum and was ready for a quiet drink with Sally in their local. Sally had been at home all day, catching up on housework and doing some weeding in the flower beds.

Greg was wearing casual trousers and a blue shirt with a woollen jumper draped over his shoulders in anticipation of the May evening becoming somewhat cooler. His dark hair was cut closely at the back and sides allowing the curls some freedom on top. Sally was wearing fawn coloured chinos with a pink blouse - the colour Greg most liked on her. Her brunette hair was tied back with a multi-coloured scrunchie. They looked around and spotted a table near the fire nook. 'You sit and I'll get the drinks,' suggested Greg.

Sally stepped towards the free table, only to be stopped in her tracks. 'Hi Sally. Good to see you. How've you been keeping?'

Sally recognised Simon's voice immediately. He and Sharon were sitting at the adjacent table.

'Well, thank you. And you?'

'Great actually. Hey, would you like to join us - for old times' sake?'

'Thanks. That would be nice.'

Some months before, Greg and Sally had been part of a pub quiz team with some others from the village. It had been fun, but after a tragedy the *Antiquarians* disbanded.

Simon pulled a chair out and Sally sat. 'How are things going?' asked Sharon.

'Same old, same old. Greg's sometimes working long hours at the museum and I'm doing my best at the Army Barracks. Afghanistan is still affecting everyone there. It's all very sad for our guys and gals serving there. But, on the brighter side, our grand-daughter, Keily, is nine. Can't believe how the time has flown.'

'You still solving mysteries?'

'Don't be silly. The only mystery I face is how it can take Greg so long to buy a couple of drinks from the bar.'

'Solved,' announced Simon, who was facing the bar and had seen Greg coming towards them, a drink in each hand.

'Hello you two,' he said as he placed the glasses on the vacant beer mats. 'Long time, no see.' He took note of Sharon, who looked radiant as usual with her blond, wavy hair falling off her shoulders, and thought, not for the first time, that it must be distracting for the male members of her congregations, to have such a pretty vicar.

'It is, but you know where I can be found every Sunday.'

'Touché.' Greg sat down. 'I do miss coming here for

the Quiz Evenings. Don't you?'

'I agree,' replied Sharon. 'They were so much fun - especially when we won.'

'Maybe, we ought to ask Terry to start them up again.'

'I think, that might bring back too many bad memories,' Simon said solemnly.

Sally changed the subject. 'Don't you find it strange coming over here, Sharon? I know you don't wear your clerical collar and all that, but most people in here know you're the vicar. It's only a few yards from your house. You could just pour yourselves drinks and avoid your parishioners. It would be cheaper too.'

'Cheaper, yes. However, I don't think I would be very good at my ministry if the only time I interacted with people was when I was in church.'

'I guess.' Sally thought for a moment. 'Don't you get irritated when people ask you things when you're 'off duty'?'

'Why would I? The conversations I have when I'm not in church and when I'm not wearing my clerical collar are some of the best.'

'Conversations about Heaven and Hell and all that stuff?'

'Not so much that, and certainly not as often as you might think. One of the things people ask is *How do you cope with doing so many funerals?* Truth is, taking a funeral is one of the most rewarding things I do. Helping someone through grief is a great privilege.'

'Oh, yes, I can understand that.'

'It is. I was thinking a bit about that earlier. I was having a conversation with someone this morning, about my predecessor, David Stainton. I'm not sure how I would cope with helping someone in his position when someone they love goes missing. In some ways not knowing must be worse that knowing. Did you know his wife?'

'Everybody knew Rebecca. She got involved in village life. Wasn't so much a customer in The Red Lion, though. She used the Post Office and shop. She helped to run a playgroup.'

'Don't forget,' added Greg, 'she worked as a Care Assistant at The Oaks Nursing Home.'

'That as well,' acknowledged Sally. 'You ought to ask some of the church members if you really want to know more. After all, we didn't know her as well as they would have done.'

'So, what do *you* think happened to her?'

'I haven't the faintest!'

'Well, I think you could take on this mystery yourselves. It's about time someone did.'

Greg looked perturbed. 'The police did a thorough investigation at the time. It's been so long - more than four years. I can't see that we'd have any better luck.'

'Come on Greg, don't be defeatist. New eyes might just be what is needed.'

'On the other hand, it might just stir things up and rekindle the pain and sadness. I wouldn't want to do that.'

'Same here,' agreed Sally.

'Well, give it some thought. Personally, I would love to know and, if you were able to solve the mystery, you would bring resolution and with that, some peace to all those involved.'

Sally and Greg looked at each other with a mutual understanding. 'Okay,' said Sally, 'we'll have a think, but we're making no promises. Now can we talk about something else?'

'Better idea,' volunteered Simon as he grabbed a pack from the shelf behind him. 'How about a game of cards?'

-o0o-

The walk back up to their home at number 62 Church Road took them just a little more than five minutes. The last vestiges of light were disappearing quickly. They had their supper watching *Britain's Got Talent*. Afterwards, with nightcaps in their hands, they made their way to bed.

'What do you think?' asked Sally.

'About what?'

'About digging into Rebecca's disappearance.'

'Oh that.'

'So, what do you think?'

Greg took a sip from his mug. 'Well... I'm not sure. On the one hand it would be wonderful to bring resolution to a mystery that's years old. On the other hand it might just stir things up without solving anything and,' he paused and took another sip, 'and we can assume that there is someone out there who knows what happened to her, someone who might not want us to find out the truth.'

'You're assuming that foul play was involved. What if

Rebecca decided to walk away? What if she experienced a fatal accident? What if she had a mental breakdown?'

'An accident which meant that her body couldn't be found after an extensive search by members of the community and the police force. A breakdown that took her off the grid!'

'I'll give you that it's unlikely, but not impossible.'

'As I said, I'm not sure we ought to take this on. What do *you* think?'

'I'm intrigued. It was the only subject of conversation for weeks after she was reported missing, even replacing the weather as the main and cherished subject of discussion. However, after a month or so, we'd moved on. When did you last have a conversation with anyone about her? Months? Years?'

'A long time, that's for sure. So, you want to go for it?'

'Yes, I'm up for asking some people a few questions and see where that leads: maybe nowhere, and if so, we can drop it and concentrate on something else.'

'Okay then. Let's do it, Sal. Where do we start?'

'Let's talk to people who best knew Rebecca and David - church members.'

'And the people she worked with.'

'Do you think we ought to gate-crash the church tomorrow?'

'I don't think that'd be gate-crashing. We know we'd receive a warm welcome from Sharon.'

'A somewhat surprised Sharon.'

'Do I have to dress up?'

'Nothing special.'

'Perhaps you should wear the mother-of-the-bride hat you had for Mark's wedding. I'd love to see you in that.'

'Stop being silly.'

Greg gulped the last of his drink, placed the mug on the bedside table and snuggled down. 'Time to sleep if we're going to church in the morning. Good night Sal. Sleep tight.'

'Sweet dreams...'

'...of lovely things.'

Sunday 6th May

3

Sunday morning found Greg and Sally making their way to St Philip's Church for the morning service, on the last minute. They both felt a bit nervous, not that it was their first time in the village church. They were, however, more used to being present for a funeral or a wedding. The double doors of the South Porch were wide open and they could hear Sharon's voice as they stepped inside.

A lady slipped out of a nearby pew and approached them. 'Good morning' she said in a whisper. She handed them some books and beckoned them to follow her as she led them to an empty pew. As they sat down, Sharon was announcing that coffee and tea would be served at the back at the end of the service. Noticing that Greg and Sally were present, she looked directly at them and continued.

'All are welcome to our service this morning, whether you're new or just visiting.' Then she announced the first hymn. The rest of the congregation stood up and the Williamses copied them.

The service continued and was not as boring as they had imagined. The service concluded by Sharon giving a blessing. As the organist began to play a stirring melody, she walked down the aisle smiling amiably at everyone as she passed. The lady who had welcomed them when they arrived, came over to them.'

'It's Mr and Mrs Williams isn't it?' They nodded. 'I've seen you here and there. Come and have a drink. You're in luck today. We even have some chocolate cake.'

'Oooo, I could kill for coffee and cake,' responded Greg.

'Not in here, please.'

Greg looked puzzled for a moment, then cracked a grin. 'Oh no. Sorry, that was the wrong thing to say wasn't it.'

They were led to a serving table laden with mugs, and plates, dainty cakes, and one massive chocolate cake.

'My name's Juliet Strange. Strange isn't it? That's got that one out of the way. I'm a churchwarden, for my sins.'

'Nice to meet you. Please call me Sally, and this is Greg.'

'Take a seat at the table over there and I'll fetch you drinks and cake. Coffees?'

'Yes please, but no cake for me. A biscuit will be fine.'

'Okeydokey. See you in a moment.'

Greg and Sally sat at a vacant table and were soon rewarded with the promised drinks. Juliet placed a plate in the centre of the table with two digestive biscuits and an enormous piece of cream-filled chocolate cake. Greg greeted the cake with wide eyes. 'No need for lunch today then!'

'Will you join us?' asked Sally.

'My pleasure. Back in moment.' Juliet slid away as

Sharon and Simon approached. Sharon had taken off her robes and was dressed in a dark blue skirt and a pale blue blouse with an attached clerical collar.

'Twice in twenty-four hours. That's a surprise. Well, welcome to my office,' Sharon said genially. 'I see Juliet is working hard to get you to come again by serving you with her chocolate cake.'

'It's bribery, if you ask me,' joked Simon.

'It's working,' said Greg as he lifted the cake to his mouth.

'We've decided to accept your challenge,' Sally declared. 'We're going to ask around and see what we can find out, though after more than four years, I doubt if we'll have much luck.'

Sharon looked downcast. 'There, and I thought you had come to hear a magnificently crafted, deeply thoughtful, provoking, yet entertaining sermon.'

'Oh. That as well,' Greg managed to say despite a mouthful of cake.

Juliet approached the table.

'Here's Juliet, so we'll leave you in her capable hands. See you again soon, I hope.'

'We'll be in touch sooner or later. Bye.'

Juliet sat down with a mug of tea as the vicar and her husband moved off to speak to others. Sally began, 'So, how long have you been a churchwarden?'

'I'm in my third year. I only agreed to fill the vacancy for one year, but Sharon is very persuasive. I hope this is my last year. I just have to find someone else to be willing to take my place.'

'I assume you weren't here when David Stainton was the vicar.'

'I wasn't churchwarden, but I knew David and Rebecca quite well. She and I used to help at the church playgroup held in the church hall, that is, when her shifts allowed it. She taught in the Sunday School as well. She was lovely.' She paused reflectively. 'It was devastating when she went missing. I remember it so well. It was on January fifteenth - a date that will stick in my mind forever. She'd been at work. That was the last time anyone saw her. She'd finished sometime in the afternoon and then she just vanished. David was phoning anyone he thought she might have called in on. Nothing! Eventually he asked people to help him look for her. Within hours there were more than a hundred people scouring the village and further afield.'

'I remember that too. Greg and I joined in with the search for as long as we could.'

'That's right. Some people didn't give up until the early hours of the next morning, and it was *so* cold. Then the police were called in. The local news, and then national news, covered the story. There were reporters and TV vans everywhere.' Juliet drank from her mug then continued. 'People came to help from near and far. Some had their theories and flooded social media with them. It gave rise to several conspiracy theories. It was horrible. Two days later, the police brought in divers to search the canal. They gave up after three days.'

'The congregation must have felt for David,'

suggested Greg.

'We did. On the following Saturday, Bishop Stephen turned up to lead a vigil in the church.'

'Oh yes. We couldn't get in because the church was already full. There were pink ribbons tied all around the church, in fact, wherever you looked in the village someone had tied a ribbon.'

'And not only in Whittlebrugh. The people of Knowle and Caulston did the same - after all David was their vicar as well.'

'So what do you think happened to Rebecca?' asked Sally.

'I've absolutely no idea. I wish I knew... for David's sake. I hope she'll turn up some day, alive. Better that she ran off with a lover than the alternative.'

'Is that possible?'

'Seriously? No way. She and David were the perfect match.'

'Some have suggested that he killed her because...'

Juliet jumped in. 'That's poppycock!' She said it so loudly that conversations around them stopped and eyes were drawn to them. Juliet glanced around, a little embarrassed then, more quietly, continued. 'People who say that, didn't know David. He was the gentlest, most gracious and loving priest you might ever meet. Anyway, why all the questions?'

'Well, that's difficult,' began Sally.

'Or not,' said Greg timidly. 'Actually it was Sharon who suggested we have a go at solving the mystery. As you probably know, we've had a bit of luck sleuthing. She challenged us to see what we could do, and we said we'd give it a go, though we think this one is probably beyond us after all this time.'

'Sharon put you up to this?'

'Well, she suggested it. She thought that, if we were able to find out what happened, it would bring... what did she say?... *resolution and peace* to everyone concerned.'

'Perhaps so. Sharon's done really well since she arrived, but things like that leave a scar on the community.'

'So is there anything else? Anything at all?'

'No. I don't think I can tell you any more than I already have.'

'What about someone else who might know something.'

'You could try old Jack Taylor. He's been a member here since he was born. He knows the church better than anyone. Officially he's still our verger, but he's just too frail to do anything strenuous any more. Gone downhill rapidly during this last year. His mind is still active. Try him, if you like.'

'Anything else?'

'Ummm, I know you mean well, and I get it that Sharon asked you, but please don't go getting peoples' hopes up just to have them crushed.'

'We'll tread carefully,' assured Sally, 'and thank you for your help.'

They looked around. They were the only ones left other than the couple of ladies behind the serving table, who were obviously waiting to finish the clearing up.

'I think it's time to go,' observed Greg. They stood up and Juliet collected up the mugs and the plate.

'Thank you, Juliet,' said Sally.

'That's okay, really. And good luck. You'll need it.'

They turned to leave, then Greg turned back. 'One last thing. Where might we find Jack Taylor?'

'He was here this morning. He lives in the almshouses on Smithy Lane. Number 5. Most often you'll spot him in the churchyard.'

'Oh! Okay.'

-o0o-

May was turning out to be a good month weather-wise. As they ambled back onto Church Road, Greg caught hold of Sally's hand. They realised that their trip to church hadn't appeared to reveal much about Rebecca Stainton and not much more about her husband.

They walked across the end of Smithy Lane and were tempted to go to the almshouses and drop in on Number 5. However, Sunday Dinner was calling and they were expecting Mark, Rosie and Keily to arrive for an afternoon visit, so meeting with Jack would have to wait.

Monday 7th May

4

Monday, being a Bank Holiday, was surprisingly pleasant so, having mixed a bit of gardening and relaxing during the day, they took an evening stroll towards the centre of the village with Debbie on her lead. They chatted about plans for holidays including a trip to Italy - a favourite destination.

At Smithy Lane they purposefully turned left and made their way to the crescent of almshouses. Sally held onto Debbie. Greg knocked on the door of Number 5. He waited for a while then knocked louder. No answer. When he turned around the door of Number 6 opened. 'You after Jack?' asked a rotund lady.

Greg walked towards her. 'Yes, we were hoping to see him.'

'You'll likely find him in the churchyard. Spends most of his time there.'

'Right. Thank you. We'll take a look.'

'That your dog?'

'Er... yes?'

'Don't let her make a mess in there or Jack'll have your guts for garters.'

'Thanks for the warning. Not to worry - she'll behave

herself.'

'Good luck then.

Greg lifted his arm – somewhere between a wave and a salute. 'Bye now.'

He caught up with Sally and they retraced their steps to Church Road and made their way through the lychgate into the churchyard. Following the path around the building, they admired the carefully-kept and recently-cut grass. They found Jack sitting on a garden bench. He had his hands resting on the end of his walking stick and appeared to be dozing. As they drew near Greg said, 'Jack Taylor I presume.'

He lifted his head and opened his eyes. 'Well I'm not David Livingstone and I'm guessing you're not Henry Stanley.'

'True. I'm Greg and this is Sally.'

'Ah, Mr and Mrs Williams, if I'm not badly mistaken.'

'Correct.'

'So what can I do for you?'

'May we sit?' asked Sally.

'Be my guest.' Sally sat on his right and Greg sat on his left. 'I feel like the jam in a sandwich,' he joked. 'Come on then, what do you want to know?'

'Well,' began Sally cautiously, 'we thought we might have a go at trying to find out what happened to Rebecca Stainton?'

'Now there's a thing. Four years and four months. Two hundred and twenty-three weeks. I think you're a bit late, don't you?'

'Better late than never.'

'Maybe. Maybe not.'

'Jack.' Greg drew Jack's attention towards him. 'What did you think of Rebecca?'

'What did *I* think of Rebecca? I'm not sure that's very important if you want to find out what happened to her.'

'We have to start somewhere.'

'Ummmm.' He paused reflectively. 'Okay. I liked her. How couldn't you? She was a pretty young thing. She busied herself in village and church life for the short time they were here. She and David suited each other. She would stop to chat with me when she was passing. Very pleasant. We hadn't had a couple at The Vicarage for a very long time so it was quite a thing when David was appointed. Now, would you know, we have a woman priest! Not like it was in days gone by when you knew what a priest was all about.'

'What do you mean?'

'Let me think.' He looked around as he was pondering how to answer. 'Do you remember Father Benedict Downley?'

'A little.'

'Now he was a *proper* priest. He knew how to make God special.'

'Special?'

'Yes. When he preached about God, you understood the wonder of the creator. You knew that you had to behave with respect for others and creation. He not only preached about God, but demonstrated it by living a devoted life.

Then Father David came with his young wife. Everything changed. You know what? He even played his guitar in church! That's not what a proper priest should do.'

'Right! But back to Rebecca. Can you think of anyone who would want to harm her?'

'No. Certainly not. It's nonsense. I never believed it had anything to do with anything she'd done. The police really messed up their investigation if you ask me. No explanation, no reason, no suspect, no body, no nothing.' Jack pulled a handkerchief from his coat pocket and blew his nose, after which he lifted his glasses and dabbed the inside corner of each of his eyes. He cleared his throat. 'It don't make no sense.'

Sally gently laid her hand on top of his. 'We want to make sense of it. I'm sure you do.'

'If someone harmed that sweet girl, then they deserve to be punished. I hope they rot in Hell.'

There was a long silence only disturbed by birdsong and Debbie panting.

Greg broke the silence. 'Thank you for speaking so openly. If we do find out anything, I promise we'll tell you.'

'Will you speak to Father David?'

'Not sure.'

'If you do, send him my regards.'

Greg and Sally stood and turned towards him. He had shut his eyes and lowered his head once more. They left him there in, what was clearly, his special place.

Wednesday 9th May

5

A phone call from Sally to The Oaks Nursing Home, arranged a meeting with the manager for 6.30pm on Wednesday.

The Williamses pulled up outside and parked in a bay marked for 'Visitors'. Greg was about to ring the doorbell of the former mansion when the front door was flung open. 'Mr and Mrs Williams, welcome to The Oaks. My name's Gordon Pitcher.' He held out his hand to shake theirs. 'Do come in.' They were led through the entrance and into the front room on the right. The bay window of the room overlooked the approach and parking area. 'Please take a seat.' He waved his hand towards a sofa. 'I'll be with you shortly. He went to his desk and picked up a phone. 'Hello Daisy. The Williamses are here. Okay?... Thanks.'

He grabbed a colourful brochure and sat in an armchair opposite the sofa. 'I'm delighted you've come to visit us. We have a wonderful establishment where we pride ourselves on the care and attention we provide for our residents. We can assure you that we will do everything possible to look after your elderly loved ones whatever their needs.'

Sally and Greg felt rather embarrassed that their

intentions for a meeting had been misconstrued. Sally spoke up. 'Oh dear, I do apologise. I think you have the wrong end of the stick.'

'Oh, so you're not looking to book a place here?'

'No. It's something quite different. Let me explain.'

At that moment there was a timid knock on the door. Gordon responded, 'Come in.'

A lady dressed in a nurse's uniform entered. 'Hello,' she said with a smile, and made directly to the second armchair.

'Daisy, this is Mr and Mrs Williams. It appears that you may not be needed after all.'

'Oh please stay,' pleaded Sally. 'I think you may be crucial to the outcome of our visit.'

Gordon leaned forward and, with obvious disappointment, discarded the brochure by dropping it onto the coffee table. 'So, how can we help you?'

'First of all, my name is Sally and this is Greg. I guess you know our vicar, Sharon Curtis.'

'Of course. She comes in now and then to visit residents and to bring Communion for those who wish it.'

'Right, well we were talking to Sharon last week and the subject of her predecessor's wife's disappearance came up.' Gordon leaned back into his chair and lifted his hands so that his fingertips were pressed together.

'A very sorry affair.'

'Indeed.' Sally continued, 'Well, she asked us, or you could say, challenged us, to see if we could shine a light on what happened to Rebecca.'

'It's, what, more than four years ago. What chance is there now?'

'We don't know. Sharon knows that we've been able to solve mysteries and puzzles in the past so...'

Greg took his turn. 'We were the ones who found Katy Mortimer when she went missing.'

'Oh yes. I thought I recognised your names, but I couldn't think why. That was tragic. We miss Katy around here.'

'We do,' added Daisy. 'She was an excellent worker and a true friend. Sadly missed by the residents and the other staff.'

'Anyway,' Sally began again, 'we know that the last time Rebecca was seen was when she left here after her shift and we wondered if you can remember anything from that day, or leading up to that day. Even the smallest thing might be significant in explaining her disappearance.'

'No.' said Gordon rather abruptly. 'I told the police detectives all that I knew, and that was nothing. She left here at the end of her shift.'

'The morning shift goes from 7.45am to 4pm,' Daisy clarified, 'so it would be sometime soon after that. Can I say, if you don't mind, a little about Rebecca.' They all nodded. 'Rebecca, as care assistant, worked directly under me in my position as nursing officer. Over the couple of years that she worked here, she was a great asset to The Oaks. She was one of the most caring people on the staff. She seemed to have a real ability and a genuine love for each resident. She would bring in little gifts for them - you know, a chocolate, or a flower she picked from the hedgerow on her way to work, little things that meant a lot. She was particularly concerned for them at the end of their journey. She was known to stay for hours with them and their family members well after her shift had finished when their time had come.'

'We don't encourage that, of course,' added Gordon.

'Correct,' she said quietly, 'but neither do we discourage it.'

'Do you have many deaths?'

'I would say 'all the time', but that would be wrong. Truth is that people who come here are most likely to leave horizontally in an ambulance or funeral director's van.'

'Luckily for us,' informed Gordon, 'we always have a waiting list.' Daisy gave him a glare. It was noted by Greg and Sally.

'Luckily for us,' Daisy repeated, 'we have a doctor nearby who will come out day or night when he's not at the surgery: Doctor Jason Edwards from the Cambridge Road Surgery in town. He lives in Knowle.'

'That's very convenient.'

'It is. He's a lovely man. You can tell he's compassionate. He has empathy for the relatives as well. On one occasion he told me that he feels deeply for them. He watched his own grandfather suffer with lung cancer. It inevitably caused breathing problems. To top it all, he developed dementia. I can see how that would shape his bedside manner. He and Rebecca seemed to be on the same wavelength.'

'I'm sure the police asked you this,' said Greg deliberately. 'Was their anyone who would want to harm Rebecca - a disgruntled relative perhaps, venting anger at a loved one's passing?'

'Yes, they asked,' replied Gordon. 'The answer remains the same. There's no one we can think of who would.'

Sally sat on the edge of the sofa in readiness to leave. 'Look, you've both been very open and helpful. This is going to be difficult. Maybe we'll never know what happened that afternoon. All we know for sure is that we lost a very special person.' She stood. The others, recognising that the visit was over, did the same. 'Thank you so much for your time.'

Gordon grabbed the brochure from the table and pressed it into Sally's hand. 'Our pleasure, and please take this. It may be useful one day.'

6

As Greg drove back through the village Sally spotted Sharon making her way to the church hall dressed in her black trousers and blouse with her clerical collar. Greg slowed down and pulled to the opposite side of the road to drive at walking pace. 'Hi Sharon. How's it going?'

Sharon bent to speak though the open window. 'Good, thank you. I'm on my way to yet another meeting - the bane of my life. How are you both?'

'We're okay. We've been asking around about Rebecca. Seems everyone remembers her as a special person. None of those we've spoken to can think of anyone who might have wanted to harm her. You've thrown us a tough one.'

'Well, I'm sorry about that. If it's too difficult...'

'No, no, no,' said Sally adamantly. 'I'm sure there must be clues to be unearthed.'

'Great. Look, sorry, must go. Don't want to be known as 'the late Reverend Curtis', do I?'

'Of course not. Though you could always blame it on us. Bye.'

Sharon straightened up, then ducked down quickly.

'Just had a thought. Have you spoken to Philip and Patricia Jones?'

'No.'

'Might be a good idea. Philip was David's churchwarden. A bit like a father figure to him, so I've heard.'

'That sounds a good idea.'

'They live on Clover Drive. Number twelve.'

'Okay, thanks. Will do.' Then she was gone.

Greg closed his window and pulled to the other side of the road to continue on the way to their home. 'It's still early,' Sally said thoughtfully, 'How about we call in to see this Philip guy?'

'Fine with me. Let's drop off the car and walk around the corner.'

'Nearly there already.'

Clover Drive backed onto Church Road and the route to it was via Caulston Road. The odd numbers of the Clover Drive were over the fence from their garden. The even numbers were on the other side of the road. Number 12 was easy to find. Even though it was still light outside, the curtains were drawn closed, with chinks of light shining through gaps. They were in two minds about knocking, but as they had come this far, they decided to give it a go anyway. They didn't have to wait long before Philip opened the door. He was wearing brown trousers, a shirt with a knitted 'tank top' and slippers. His thinning, silver hair was cut short.

'Hello?'

'Hello. Mr Jones?'

'Yes.'

'I'm Greg. This is Sally.'

'I saw you on Sunday at St Philip's didn't I?'

'You did.'

'What can I do for you?'

'May we come in?' asked Sally with a winsome smile. 'If you're busy we could come back another time.

'I don't see why not. Is this church business?'

'Kind of.'

'Intriguing. Come in.'

He led them into the front room and introduced them to his wife, Patricia. He turned the TV off and invited them to sit. Patricia offered them a cup of tea. They accepted and she went to brew a pot.

'So what's this all about?'

'Sharon's given us a quest.'

'I wonder what the vicar's up to now.'

Sally drew a breath. 'She wants us to try and discover what happened to Rebecca Stainton.'

'Oh!' He raised his eyebrows.

'Sharon suggested we speak to you. You were David's churchwarden weren't you?'

'I was. I was churchwarden when he was appointed, so I was one of those who interviewed him. He was just what we needed, a young, enthusiastic priest with a desire to see the church grow. Frankly, his predecessor should have retired some time before. He was tired. Not as old as me, but old nevertheless.'

Patricia returned with a tray full of tea cups, saucers, plates, biscuits, milk, sugar and a steaming teapot. She placed it on a side table where she began to pour the tea. With Philip's help they were all soon sitting comfortably, drinking their tea.

'Where were we? Ah yes.' Philip turned his head towards his wife. 'Pat, dear, Greg and Sally want to know about Rebecca. I was telling them about David when you brought in the tea.' He turned his head towards them. 'Rebecca was a sweetie. She was kind, generous with high morals. She was known to speak out on behalf of children caught up in war zones, communities around the world who lived without fresh, clean water or sanitation...'

Patricia butted in. '...human trafficking, the need to protect elephants from ivory hunters, fair trade, and so much more.'

Philip continued. 'Both of them were fervent supporters of mission organisations in this country and aboard.'

'Do you know how they met?' asked Sally.

'Yes we do. They shared a lot with us. I know vicars don't usually have special friends in their parishes. No one would want it thought that there were favourites amongst the congregation after all. However, I can say we had a special relationship with David and Rebecca. It was, I think, more paternal. He knew he could ask me anything or tell me anything. We spent many an evening chatting together. I witnessed some of their happiest, saddest, frustrating and...' Philip sighed, '...loneliest moments.' He paused for a moment in reflection.

'You were going to tell them how they met,' prompted Patricia.

'Right. They met in Cambridge when David was at theological college. She was a member of the parish where David was on placement during his second year. By the middle of his third year they were engaged. They married at the end of his last term. Their first home was in the parish where he served his curacy. Whittlebrugh was his first living.'

Sally looked puzzled. 'They sound as if they were the perfect couple.'

'Perfect? I don't think there is such a thing as a *perfect* couple. They didn't agree about everything. Nothing serious you know.' Philip hurried on. 'They knew how not to let differences spoil their relationship or linger.'

'Did they have any problems?'

'What, you mean like living on a stipend; like not being able to have children; like Rebecca being on the other side of the country from her parents and her siblings; like parishioners not welcoming David's style of ministry? Yes, they had some problems, but they faced them together.'

Greg found one thing particularly interesting. 'What do you mean about the parishioners?'

'This is not something I'm proud of as a long-standing church member, and I wouldn't want it splashed around. There were some of the older members who didn't want their church being modernised with new songs and new prayers. Less *Thees* and *Thous*! The Knowle congregation was perhaps the worst. Their motto is still *As it was in the beginning, is now, and ever shall be.*'

'Now dear,' chided Patricia, 'you mustn't be too hard on them. It was only a few.'

Philip responded firmly. 'They were a *vocal* few. Still are for that matter. I suspect that those vocal few were plotting to get David out. They were happy with Father Dominic. He did things *their* way.'

'You can't be saying that a plot might have involved Rebecca?'

'No. I'm sure that would be far beyond their moral limitations. I couldn't guess what they might do apart from writing a letter or two to the Bishop.'

Sally was thinking about something else Philip had said. 'You mentioned that they couldn't have children. Was that widely known?'

'No, and I'd be grateful if you didn't speak of that to anyone else. It kind of slipped out, for which I'm ashamed. I've probably broken a confidence in even mentioning it. However, you'll understand that finding out was one of the lowest points of their time at The Vicarage. I'm sure that had nothing to do with what happened later.'

'Did you see David much after Rebecca went missing?' asked Greg.

'I did, or to be more precise, *we* did. We spent many hours with him. He was unable to take services, what with his own trauma to deal with and the hordes of press and media people around. Bishop Stephen found him a job at Lakeside, the Diocesan Retreat and Conference Centre near

Stone. For several months he was officially their chaplain. In actual fact, I think he was put there to be supported rather than to help. Patricia and I helped him pack the contents of The Vicarage up. Most of them went into storage. After a while he was appointed to a parish in Yorkshire - a fresh, new start. We still keep in touch.'

'How's he doing?'

'Okay, I think. He's changed. He's not the same man who came here. Not surprisingly, he's more somber nowadays.'

'So what do you think happened to Rebecca?'

'God only knows.'

'Or maybe someone else does?'

'Yes,' Philip murmured, 'maybe someone else does.'

Recognising that they had probably learned as much as they were going to learn from Philip, Sally made to leave. 'Thank you for your time. We've taken up too much of it already.'

As they stood, Patricia suddenly spoke up. 'Wait a moment. I want to show you something.' She hastened from the room. They could hear her climbing the stairs and then returning. In her hands she held an unusual teddy bear. 'Rebecca gave me this,' she said as she showed it to them. The bear was in a sitting position with its head bowed and its arms folded together. 'It's a sad bear isn't it? She told me it represented how she felt at the time. But she told me she was looking forward to a better time. It was, she said, her Christian hope. I think her experience was something that made her value *all* life so dearly.'

Friday 11th May

7

Bags of shopping from the regular Friday supermarket trip, were lying on the kitchen worktop waiting to be unpacked when Greg's mobile rang. Sally continued to transfer frozen items from the bags into the freezer while Greg answered the call. 'Hello,' he said in his best non-committal 'phone answering' voice.

'Good evening,' came the man's reply. 'Am I speaking to Greg Williams?'

'May I know who's asking?'

'It's Philip, Philip Jones. We met the other evening.'

'Oh hello, yes, it's Greg here. Sorry about that, you never know who might be calling. How can I help?'

'I hope you don't mind, I had a word with the vicar to make sure you were 'kosher'. Anyway she assured me you were.'

'Good to know.'

'Yes well.... So, Patricia and I were talking after you left and there's something you might not know - something that might be useful. It would have been Rebecca's birthday tomorrow.'

'Okay,' he said, uncertain how the information might be of any use.

'The thing is that for the last few years, ever since she went missing, her family have visited Whittlebrugh on her birthday. In the past they've brought flowers, tied with pink ribbons, and placed them near the gate of The Oaks Nursing Home. I expect they'll probably do the same tomorrow, leaving birthday cards there as in previous years.'

'Really.'

'I'm sure you already know that the last time she was seen was when she was leaving there after work. So, Patricia thought you might like to meet them.'

'Wow. Thank you. Do you know what time they're likely to be around?'

'I think it's in the middle of the day.'

'I'm working tomorrow, but Sally may be able to go and see if she can meet them.'

'Well, we hope it works out for you. We certainly would like to know what happened to Rebecca. We've never stopped praying for her and for David.'

'Again, thank you for that. Oh, and you might say one for us as well.'

'Of course. Our pleasure. Goodnight and good luck.'

'Thanks. Bye.' Greg ended the call.

'What was all that about?' asked Sally.

'To cut a long story short, that was Philip Jones. Could you possibly go into the village tomorrow around lunchtime and see if you can meet up with Rebecca's parents? It's her birthday and they've been visiting each year. Apparently, if they turn up tomorrow, they'll lay flowers and leave birthday cards.'

'Oh! Okay? What do they look like? What are their names? Why?'

Greg huffed. 'No idea what they look like. Don't know their names. Why? Well you might find out something from them that we don't know.'

'If I'm to do this, at the very least, I could do with knowing their names.'

'I'll call Philip back. Hold on.' Sally returned to the unpacking and Greg checked the call history and made the call. At the end he told Sally that their surname was Bailey. 'One other thing,' he told Sally, 'they'll probably be carrying a bouquet tied with pink ribbons, to lay by the gates of The Oaks. Philip said they would probably leave birthday cards as well.'

As Sally considered this new information, she tried to imagine what it must be like to lose a daughter or a sister in such a dramatic way. She thought that the uncertainty must chew at them. Obviously, the Baileys decided that they would try to keep hope by making this annual pilgrimage to Whittlebrugh. If Sally could do something to help, then she would, but she had no idea how that would turn out.

Saturday 12th May

With such scant information, Sally left the house just before half-past-eleven. She called in at the village shop and bought some stamps from the Post Office counter. There were quite a few people around, some she knew, some she recognised and some she didn't. She could hear children playing in the playground on Canal Road, behind the shop. She felt rather conspicuous just standing around and when she saw the village gossip, Mrs Talbot, heading towards her, she crossed the road and hid in the lychgate. It struck her that she didn't know Mrs Talbot's Christian name and wondered how many people did.

A few cars passed in each direction and the Stafford bus went by without stopping. After half-an-hour Sally decided to wander down the road towards The Oaks. She stayed on the pavement as the curve of the road meant that the visibility for drivers was quite restricted.

After a few minutes she arrived at the temporary fencing surrounding the building site of the new estate. The land had been sold to the developer by the owners of the nursing home. It was to be known as Oaks Close. A section of the original Oak Hall boundary wall, had been removed so that a new roadway could give access for construction traffic. Mud from the site was splattered onto the road by the vehicles leaving the site.

She continued walking and found herself approaching a parked car. Up ahead she could see the backs of three people: two men and a woman. Sally instinctively knew that this *was* the Bailey family. She approached closer before drawing their attention.

'Excuse me.' The family turned to face her and stepped to the side so as to allow her to pass. The woman was holding a bouquet of pink flowers tied with a wide, pink florist's ribbon. 'Hello,' Sally started. 'I don't wish to disturb you, but I did want to meet you. May I introduce myself?' They looked flummoxed. 'My name is Sally Williams. I presume you are Rebecca's family.'

'We are,' confirmed the younger of the two men. 'What is it to you? You're not a journalist are you, Sally?'

'No I'm not. Let me explain. This may sound impertinent, but I was hoping to speak with you about Rebecca. Like so many people in Whittlebrugh, we're still looking for answers. We believe too much time has gone without resolution.'

The older man stared at her coldly. 'And you think you can solve the mystery when detectives couldn't? Fat chance!'

'Dad,' said the younger man, 'at least someone is still looking. Rebecca hasn't been forgotten.'

'How did you find us?' asked the lady Sally now assumed to be Mrs Bailey.

'Philip Jones told us you might be here today.'

'Philip, the churchwarden?'

'Yes, though he's no longer a churchwarden.'

The younger man spoke again. 'Look, Sally, we've come to lay some flowers. It's a very personal thing for us. We still cling to the hope that we'll see my sister again, hence the pink flowers and ribbon. Would you mind giving us a few minutes then, perhaps, we might give you some time? Okay?'

'Of course. I'm sorry if I've disturbed you.'

Without another word, the Baileys turned and

walked to the open gateway. Sally watched as Rebecca's father tied the bouquet to the bars of the wrought-iron gate. They interlaced large envelopes into the bars. These, Sally guessed, would be birthday cards, as Philip had predicted. For a moment they stood in silence with their heads bowed. Mr Bailey said a prayer. Sally couldn't hear the words, but they chorused an 'Amen' at the end. They hugged each other closely before stepping away and walking somberly back towards her.

'Sally,' said the young man when they reached her, 'my name is Joshua, though everybody, bar Mom and Dad, call me Josh. I'm the youngest of the family. Rebecca was..., *is* my big sister. I have another sister, Sarah, who is a little older than me. She couldn't come with us this time. I think you realise that these are our parents.' He waved his arm towards them.

Sally smiled, 'I'm so glad to meet you. My husband and I remember the day Rebecca went missing. We joined in the search. I seem to recall you attended the vigil in the church. We were there, though there were so many people we had to stand outside.'

'Thank you,' said Mrs Bailey graciously.

'I wish we could have done more, Mrs Bailey.'

'Please call me Mary and this is my husband, Robert. At least you tried.'

'We're off to find some lunch,' explained Mr Bailey, 'and then we're heading back home.'

'May I ask, where is home?'

'It's a village just north of Cambridge. You've

probably never heard of it: Histon, once known for jams and jellies.'

'Sorry, no. Have you ever eaten at The Red Lion? They do an excellent lunch.'

'No. We've never felt like staying around for too long.'

'I can recommend it, and if you were in agreement, perhaps I could eat with you. That way I could find out more about Rebecca.'

Mr Bailey looked at his wife and son for their reaction. They both nodded. 'Seems like we have a plan. Jump in. We'll give you a lift.'

8

For Cliff, Saturday morning gave him another chance to try out his new hobby. He persuaded Tony to meet him again by the canal bridge on Knowle Lane. When Tony arrived Cliff was, once more, on the south side of the bridge and had unpacked the equipment onto the towpath.

Tony greeted him. 'Morning, Cliff. I hope we have better luck today.'

'Morning. I've a really good feeling about this.'

'I admire your optimism. Not falling in the water would be a success for me.'

'Come on Tony. I'll give you the first throw.'

Tony pulled a pair of heavy duty, waterproof gloves from his back pocket and pulled them on, watched by his impressed friend. He took the rope and tossed the magnet into the middle of the canal. He pulled on the rope and it came easily to the surface. He lifted it out and was surprised to find that something was attached.

While Tony held the magnet, Cliff prised off a knife and a coin. He rubbed the coin. 'Our first piece of any value – a 2008 two pence piece. Try again.'

Tony's second throw was diagonal, and to the other

side of the canal. When they retrieved the magnet, they had recovered a washer about two inches diameter,. and a cold chisel.

Cliff took over, though his first throw was delayed by a passing narrow boat. When the boat was clear, his throw recovered a garden parasol without the cloth. His next one brought out a frying pan and a six-inch nail still embedded in a chunk of wood. The next throw brought out a crow bar.

'Let's try on the north side of the bridge,' suggested Tony.

'Okay with me.' They collected their finds and climbed back up to the road, crossed it, and returned to the towpath on the other side.

'Your turn, Tony.'

The search continued and they pulled up several items including a couple of low-value decimal coins, a child's scooter, two spoons and a fork, an old key and, most exciting, a cash box. The box was locked but they managed to rip it open using the recovered crow bar and the knife. Their excitement turned to disappointment when all it contained, as Tony had predicted, was a wad of wet till receipts. After that, they gave up, packed up everything and returned to the village in Cliff's car.

'How about a drink?' asked Tony.

'Sure,' said Cliff, who pulled into The Red Lion parking area.

- o 0 o -

Robert, Mary, Josh and Sally found a table in the

restaurant at the rear of The Red Lion. Sally knew this room quite well as it was also used as a function room. They placed their orders for lunch and were sipping their drinks as they waited. To Sally, it felt just a little awkward, as if she were intruding on a family's mourning. She wanted to ask a question but didn't know how to phrase it. In the end she settled on one option. 'Which birthday are you celebrating today?'

'Rebecca's thirty-fifth. Not so much of a celebration. If we had Rebecca here, we would have a pink cake covered with pink candles.'

'She loved pink,' explained Robert. 'Ever since she was a little girl, she loved dressing up in pink. Sometimes she would be a fairy complete with wings and a wand. She was so cute.' Robert looked away wistfully. 'She never lost her love of pink.'

'That's why,' added Josh, 'when David told us that local people had suggested tying yellow ribbons around the village, like in that song, we suggested 'pink' ribbons instead.'

'There are still a few to be seen,' said Sally brightly. 'They don't look so pink any more. They've faded and become somewhat dirty. However, I can assure you that people haven't forgotten her. It was actually our new vicar who challenged my husband, Greg, and me to see if we could solve the mystery of her disappearance.'

'Are you private detectives?' asked Robert.

Sally laughed. 'No, not at all. We've been caught up in some awful dramas and somehow managed to solve the mysteries. Sharon, our vicar, was involved in a recent one. It involved a death and a mystery. That's why she thought we might take a look. Silly really, as Rebecca's disappearance was so long ago and the police couldn't find any trace back then.'

'Are you hopeful?'

'There's always hope when there's no certainty.'

'And sometimes clues take a while to surface.'

'True. We've only been on this for a week. We've had a few conversations and all we've learned is how sweet and caring Rebecca was.'

'And intelligent and pretty.'

'You know,' said Mary timidly, 'I'm really pleased someone is interested in doing something. It would be horrible to think that Rebecca had gone and no one was bothering to find her. You will keep looking for her, won't you?'

'We'll do our best.'

Their meals arrived and the conversation changed to other things. They spoke about David and his new parish and the journey home to Cambridgeshire. Robert informed her that it would take them about two-and-a-half hours. Sally told them where she worked and about Greg's work at Stafford Museum. They showed some interest in the museum and promised to visit it on another occasion.

After the dessert dishes were cleared away Sally decided to have another go to find out anything she could from the Baileys. 'Can you tell me any more about Rebecca? You never know, there maybe something that could help us.'

'Like what?' said Josh,

'I don't know.... You must have spoken to her during the days and weeks beforehand.'

'We spoke on the phone every Sunday evening.' Mary replied. 'I didn't sense anything different. She was enjoying parish life and her work. She was certainly happy to be with David.'

'Mary!' Robert was looking at her knowingly.

She hesitated, then responded. 'I don't think that's important, Robert.'

'Maybe it is, maybe it isn't. Perhaps Sally should decide that for herself.' He took a deep breath. 'They'd found out that they couldn't have children of their own. As you can imagine, they were struggling with that.'

Sally saw that Mary's eyes were welling up. 'Yes, we heard about that from Philip. He thought they were dealing with it very well.'

'If there was something she was worried about,' said Mary, 'I'm sure she would have told me, or David, or her diary.'

'She kept a diary?'

'Yes. She wrote in it every day. She started when she was about ten. I remember because she was at the end of her last year at primary school. She asked for a diary for her birthday. Said it would help her with her spelling.'

'And she was still keeping it after all these years?'

'Every night. When she disappeared, David let me read it, one of the police detectives too. Neither of us found anything strange or suspicious.'

Robert began to be unsettled. 'Sally, I hope you don't mind, but I really think we ought to be on our way. You never know if the roads will be clear. I don't trust the M6.'

'Of course.' She continued apologetically. 'I'm sorry to have kept you. Thank you for sharing your meal with me.'

They all stood and Robert gave Sally his mobile and home telephone numbers 'just in case'. In return Sally gave her numbers to him.

As they walked through the Bar to the main entrance a local man was handing Terry, the landlord, a big old key. Sally heard him tell Terry that he'd fished it out of the canal and that he thought it would look great hung on a beam with the other keys Terry had collected and displayed.

They left The Red Lion and Sally waved them off as she wondered if she'd ever see them again. *All depends on if we find Rebecca, dead or alive.*

9

Debbie was waiting for her and, as usual, made a fuss. It was obvious that she wanted to go for a walk, so Sally attached her lead and the next hour was spent walking around the village, first by Caulston Road and then onto Honeysuckle Lane returning to the village centre on Smithy Road.

Sally loved May. In fact she considered May her favourite month. The hedgerow was full of colour with blossoms; bright yellow buttercups punctuated the lush green grass of the verges; butterflies danced on the breeze; and birds sang their songs for all to hear.

On this particular day, her thoughts were centred, not so much on what was around her, but on the mystery of Rebecca's disappearance. Meeting the Bailey family had focused her mind more sharply. As she walked she considered all that she had gleaned in the last week. It seemed meager in terms of solving the mystery. They had learned much about Rebecca's character, though little about what might have led to her disappearance. *What happened to her? If dead, where is her body? If alive, where did she go?*

As she continued walking, she noticed one of the faded pink ribbons tied to one of the bars on the school fence. She stopped for a moment and looked at it. It seemed to her to look forlorn and without hope. And yet that was the opposite of what the Baileys intended. They wanted pink to represent hope, hope that Rebecca would be found alive. That was less likely as each day, each month, each year was crossed off on the calendar.

'Penny for your thoughts.' Sally turned to face Jack Taylor.

'You made me jump.' Jack was leaning on his walking stick. Debbie was wagging her tail and sniffing around his shoes.

'Sorry, I didn't mean to frighten you. I saw you from my window.' He nodded towards his home across the road. 'You looked as if you were frozen to the spot.'

'Oh!'

'Everything all right?'

'I guess.'

'Still thinking about Rebecca?'

'Yes.'

'A miserable tragedy. Not many pink ribbons left are there?'

'No.'

'Someone once told me that there is always a simple solution to every complex problem... and it's always wrong.'

'I wish I had a simple solution. There isn't even that.'

'Keep at it, young lady, for the sake of all those who knew her. She deserves a champion.'

'We seem to be getting nowhere. Perhaps it's time to quit and let someone else take up the challenge.'

'No. No. I'll tell you this: At your end, you'll regret the things you didn't do more than the things you did do.'

Sally looked at the old bow on the fence. 'I don't know who we should turn to next. It's all so long ago.'

'When you're my age, a few years is a short time. I was born between the wars. My father fought in North Africa. I remember the end of the war and him coming home a sad, melancholy man. In later life, he used to come down to the churchyard to stare at the names on the War Memorial. Losing someone, in his case comrades, can change your life.' He stood silently. Sally kept quiet in respect. He shook his head as if coming back to the present.

'There are people who will never be the same because of what happened on January fifteenth. Let that be your reason. It's not a game you're playing, it's a crusade to bring justice for David and *her* family. Perhaps you should do something to re-awaken the memories of the people of this parish. Someone must know something.' He paused. 'Anyway, you've heard enough from an old man who wished he were younger, like you are, who wished he could do more. See you around.'

With that, he turned on his heel and ambled back across the road leaning heavily on his stick, leaving Sally deep in thought. Eventually she snapped out of her reflection. 'Come on Debbie, let's go home.'

-o0o-

Greg's day at the museum had been much the same as usual, except for a group of young teenagers who had decided that the museum was an appropriate place to play

Hide and Seek. He spent a while searching for them and expelling them from the building. Thankfully none of the exhibits had been damaged. Then, as he was locking up, the security system played up. He was irritated because he had to reset system and test the alarm. Neither of these things had put him in a good mood. Sally rang him and asked him to pick up a takeaway from the Chinese on his way home.

As soon as Sally heard the noise of the car coming up the drive, she filled their wine glasses with their favourite white wine. Debbie trotted to the front door to greet Greg.

'In here,' called Sally from the kitchen.

'Coming.' Greg dropped the takeaway plastic bag on the worktop. 'I'm off upstairs to change.' He turned and left the room brusquely.

Sally raised her eyebrows at his demeanor. She served their meals onto plates, taking her own, and her drink, through to the living room. She made herself comfortable on the sofa with her plate on her lap. She had turned on the TV and was watching the beginning of the Eurovision Song Contest by the time Greg entered the room in a dressing gown.

'Where's mine?' he asked.

'On the worktop as usual, with your drink.' Greg collected his plate and glass and plonked himself onto his seat next to Sally. 'What's wrong with you?'

'Nothing really, just fed up.'

'Why? Oh wait. I want to see this.' She turned the TV sound up a notch to watch Ukraine's entry - the first song. Three minutes later she turned the sound down again. 'Go on then, why are you fed up?'

'I don't know.' he said without enthusiasm. 'Work wasn't great, then some stupid driver cut me up. Usual stuff.'

'Well, you're home now. Time to relax. Day off tomorrow. We can go to bed early. You can get some well-earned rest. Do you want to hear about my day?'

Greg had just taken a mouthful of Chicken Kung Po so she waited for him to swallow and sip his wine before he answered in a less than encouraging way. 'Okay.'

'Right, so I met Mr and Mrs Bailey with their son Josh. They had just arrived near the gates of The Oaks Nursing Home. They tied a bouquet to the fence and left some birthday cards. Then we had lunch at The Red Lion. They obviously want to know what happened to Rebecca. Robert even gave me his phone numbers so we can keep in touch.'

'Did you find out anything important?'

'Not sure that you could say that there was anything *important*, but I've learnt more about Rebecca.'

'Well, I think we should pack it in. The professionals have given up. Did you know there are about a hundred thousand adults who go missing every year in the UK of which there are about a thousand that are never heard of again, dead or alive? I've been looking it up.'

'No, I didn't know that. Wow!'

'Frankly we're wasting our time. If she wanted to go missing then she's done it well. If someone murdered her, and disposed of her body, they've done it well. Either way we're on a wild goose chase.'

'But what about David and the Baileys, and everyone else who knew her and loved her?' Sally pleaded. 'They're in limbo until the truth is known.'

'Let them hire a private detective if the police won't do anything more.'

'We can do this.'

'No, we can't. You're a fool to think we can.' He put his empty plate on the coffee table. 'I'm off to bed,' he blurted as he left his astonished wife staring after him.

She stayed up to watch the end of Eurovision. She decided, even that was better than facing Greg in a bad, negative mood. The UK came twenty-fourth of twenty-six. *There's a surprise! At least we didn't score nil points.* Greg was fast asleep when Sally made her way to bed. In the circumstances, she was relieved.

Sunday 13th May

10

The bad mood extended into the morning. Greg, who would normally have made them a coffee each to drink in bed, was pretending to sleep, so Sally decided to leave him be for the time being.

She put the duster over and whipped around with the vacuum cleaner before making herself a coffee. She flicked though the junk mail that had arrived in the post during the week and dropped it in the bin. At ten-thirty she made Greg a coffee, put it on his bedside table before grabbing her clothes and taking a leisurely shower. While the water pummelled her skin, she reflected on what Jack had said about re-awakening the memories of people. *Maybe Greg was right in one aspect. They probably couldn't solve the mystery by themselves, but perhaps they could if the community backed them.*

When she returned to the bedroom, Greg was sitting up in bed. 'Good morning, Greg.'

'Morning,' he replied grouchily.

'Did you sleep well?'

'Not too bad.'

'How do you feel?'

'Okay.'

'Come on Greg, we can't go through the day like this.

It would be nice to have a proper conversation. You can't be grumpy for ever.' No response.

'I've been thinking.... You're probably right about one thing.' Greg looked at her with an inquisitive expression on his face. Sally explained: 'We can't find out what happened to Rebecca by ourselves.' His face brightened as he felt vindicated. 'So,' she continued, 'we need help.'

'Oh. You still want us to carry on.'

'I do. I want to find out what happened to Rebecca so that those who knew and loved her can be released from their state of limbo; so that they can properly get on with their lives.'

'I get that. Who's going to help, then?'

'Everyone.' Greg laughed at the idea. 'Well not everyone. I didn't tell you that I saw Jack again yesterday on Smithy Road. I was out walking Debbie and stopped outside the school when I noticed an old pink bow tied to the fence. Jack came over and we had a chat. He suggested we remind people about Rebecca. Most people will have put her disappearance to the back of their minds. Someone, somewhere must know something.'

'How would you do that?'

'I haven't figured that out yet.'

'You'd need some publicity.'

'I don't think the Stafford Mail would be interested unless there was some new information.'

'I'll give it some thought.'

'So, you're back on track?'

'Not sure yet. We'll see.'

'Right, get yourself dressed and we'll go out somewhere nice. I think a distraction might even inspire us.'

Sally sat at the dressing table and worked on her hair as Greg made his way to the bathroom.

-o0o-

A three-and-a-half hour walk at Hawkstone Park to see the follies with Debbie in tow, was certainly a distraction. The Grotto, Swiss Bridge, Raven's Shelf views, Sir Rowland Hill's Monument, the White Tower, the Hermitage, not to mention Dragon's Wood and Rhododendron Jungle, were mind blowing.

They returned to Whittlebrugh on a route that took them by back roads through the countryside. The last stretch brought them through Knowle village. Sally rested her eyes for most of the journey.

Debbie, who was riding in the back, knew she was near home as Greg approached their drive. She stood up and started moving from side to side. Sally opened her eyes as she came out of her 'car sleep'. They came to a stop, exited the car and made their way indoors tired and hungry.

While rice was being cooked on the hob, Sally heated up some chilli con carne she had put away from a triple batch she'd made on a previous occasion. Greg prepared Debbie's tea and laid places in the kitchen. Soon they were tucking into their meal.

'You were probably asleep when we came over the canal,' stated Greg.

'I was only half asleep and, actually, I was aware of

the bump as we crossed the bridge.'

'Then you wouldn't have seen what I saw.'

'Clearly not. I had my eyes shut,' she admitted. 'What did you *see*?'

'You know the railings at the end of the stonework - the ones separating the road from the steps down to the towpath.'

'Yes.'

'Well, I spotted one.'

'Don't be so obtuse, Greg. One what?'

'Pink bow. It was tied to the railings.'

'Oh. So there are at least two left.'

'Probably a few more, if you're looking out for them.'

'Probably. I guess most people don't see them, as the ones that are left are just part of the scenery.'

'Well, how about this for an idea? How about putting some new ones up in the village? That would remind everybody about Rebecca.' Sally put her fork down, turned to Greg and gave him a big kiss. 'What's that for?' said her astonished husband.

' 'Cos I love you and I think that's a fabulous idea. That would be a great way to publicise, to remind everyone about her disappearance.'

'Thank you.'

Sally's mind was racing. 'Right. At lunch break tomorrow, would you pop into the florist's in High Street and buy some pink florists' ribbon. Blow that. Buy a reel of it. We'll cut it into pieces and make ribbons. Yes! And we'll write 'Rebecca' on each ribbon. We can tie them up. We can ask Mrs Young at the school if she'd involve the children. Oh, and we could ask Sharon to get the congregation of St Philip's to put some up. I'm sure they'd be happy to help.' She continued excitedly. 'When the place is covered in pink ribbons, surely the Stafford Mail will take notice.'

'Stop,' Greg snapped.

'Don't you like the idea.'

Greg smiled. 'I think it might well work so... forget a reel of ribbon, let's order several from Amazon. Oh, and by the way...'

'Yes?'

'I love you too.'

The plates were left on the draining board as Greg and Sally had other things on their mind.

-o0o-

The ribbon arrived on Tuesday. After their evening meal, they sat in the kitchen trying various ways of making the ribbons up. They discovered that the 50 millimeters-wide polypropylene ribbon, tore lengthwise very easily. So they cut it into 500mm lengths and tore it in half, allowing Sally to fashion two bows from each section.

They continued through the evening until the first reel was empty. To finish them off, they tore two hundred lengths of 5mm wide and threaded these through the back, so the bows could be attached to railings, fences, trees, gates or whatever. Finally, they wrote Rebecca's name on each one and filled a large cardboard box with the finished product.

'Great job,' said Greg wearily.

'We did well, and there's more ribbon if we need it.'

'Do you realise what time it is?'

Sally checked her watch. 'What!' She stood up quickly. 'It's nearly two o'clock. We've got to get up in the morning.'

'Half day for me.'

'You still have to be at work for the first half. Come on let's call it a day.'

'Well, let's call it Wednesday, because it already is.'

Wednesday 16th May

11

Mrs Susan Young had been the Headteacher at St Philip's Church of England Primary School for four years. Having worked her way up to leader of Key Stage Two in a Stafford primary school, and still in her twenties, she was appointed as Deputy Head.

Four years later, the then Headteacher of the Whittlebrugh school, retired. Susan, along with several other teachers from other schools, applied for the vacant position. Impressed, not only with her record at St Philip's, but also by her confident and comprehensive interview answers, she was appointed.

She was still in her thirties, though she looked much younger. That's how parents had given Susan Young the nickname *So Young*. Nevertheless, she had the respect of staff, governors and parents alike.

Sitting at her desk on Wednesday morning, the school secretary put a call through to her.

'Good morning. Mrs Young speaking.' She pushed hair behind her left ear.

'Good morning. My name is Greg Williams. I wonder if I might meet with you later on today. I have a suggestion to put to you.'

'I'm really quite busy today. Is it important?'

'To me, and to my wife, it is. We think it's something which the children of your school could get involved with, for the benefit of the Whittlebrugh community.'

'I have a staff meeting after school, but... I could give you fifteen minutes at 3pm.'

'That would be great. Thank you. See you at three.'

'My pleasure. Bye.'

She put the receiver down. She was sure she knew the name: Greg Williams. She wondered whether he had been a parent of a former pupil. *Greg Williams?*

The idea of doing things to benefit the community was attractive. She knew that one of the things the Ofsted inspectors looked for and liked, was community engagement. She hoped Greg's suggestion was one they could be proud of, and one that would fulfill that item of the inspection.

A tap on the door interrupted her train of thought. 'Come in,' she called.

-o0o-

Susan had to deal with an emergency during the afternoon. *How was it that there was an emergency nearly every day*, she thought. As three o'clock approached, she was still dealing with an angry parent. The school bell rang for the end of the school day and the parent decided that she had better go to the gate and collect her daughter. *Thank goodness.*

Susan ushered her out and caught the eye of Mr Williams sitting in a chair in the lobby with a visitor's badge lanyard slung around his neck. 'Sorry. Be with you in a moment.' As promised, a moment later she returned. Greg stood to greet her. 'Good afternoon Mr Williams.'

'Good afternoon. Nice to meet you.'

'My pleasure, come in.' She led him into her office and invited him to sit on a chair in front of her desk. 'First of all, I'd like to apologise for the delay. I had an important matter to deal with. However, I'm with you now, so let's get down to it. How can we help you?'

'Well... okay.... I'm sure you remember when the vicar's wife, Rebecca, went missing.'

'Indeed I do. A terrible time for all concerned.'

'It certainly was.'

'Is there any news?'

'No, and that's the point. Sharon Curtis challenged us, that is Sally and me, to see if we could investigate her disappearance. As far as the police are concerned, it appears to be a 'cold case' with no resources given to it. After more than four years that's not too surprising.'

'Agreed. Got it!'

'Sorry?'

'Greg and Sally Williams. You were involved with the case surrounding our teaching assistant, Nicola Chambers, weren't you?'

'We were. Thank goodness that's all over.'

'Less said the better. So, what on earth can the school do to help with your 'challenge'?'

'You'll remember the pink ribbons that appeared all over the village.

'Of course.'

'They were a powerful symbol of hope when there was little hope. There are a few faded ones left, but most have gone. Actually, on the way in, I did notice one of the few originals tied to your school fence.'

'Really? I don't remember seeing it.'

'And that's the point. We think that if we're going to find new information, we need to remind everyone about Rebecca's disappearance. If we can have new pink bows tied around Whittlebrugh, and if we can raise some publicity, perhaps someone will come forward with information - something that they now remember, something that, at the time, seemed insignificant.'

'So...?'

'So, we have made some pink bows and wondered if you could give them out to your children to take home and display them on their gates or wherever they'll be seen.'

'Oh. That might be possible. We wouldn't like to delve too deep into the event.... No. Why not? I think I'd better run it by the Chair of Governors first, otherwise I think we can do that.' Susan was getting more excited at the proposition. 'We could probably do an assembly about 'hope' without going into too many details. We'd need those bows.'

'How many would you need?'

'One for each child. That's one hundred and thirty-seven.'

'Oh!'

'Is that a problem?'

'No. That's amazing. I've brought a box full of bows with me. There are two-hundred.'

'Great. May we have them all? I'm sure we could distribute them. You'll have to give us a few days and it'll be done.'

'That's fantastic. All we need to do then, is arrange for some posters to invite people to contact us if they have information to help us find out what happened to Rebecca.'

'By the way, our children come from Whittlebrugh, Knowle, Caulston and other places in the wider area. So there'll be pink bows all over the place.'

'Wow! Even better.'

Susan stood up. 'I must dash.' She came around the desk, opened the door and led Greg out into the lobby. 'Please see our secretary and sign out before you leave.' She glanced around and spotted Greg's cardboard box. 'Is that the bows?' He nodded. 'Leave it with me. Bring in a poster when you have one and we'll copy it and get those out as well.'

'Thank you again.' They shook hands.

'My pleasure. Good luck.'

-o0o-

When Sally came in from work, Greg and Debbie were both waiting for her as she drove her Fiat 500 onto the driveway. Debbie jumped up to greet her, Greg gave her a kiss. 'I have some bad news about the bows we made.'

'What's wrong?' Sally was clearly disappointed.

'I met with Mrs Young at the school as we had discussed.'

'And she wouldn't help?'

'Oh yes, she'll help. The problem is she wanted all two-hundred, so now we have to make some more for the church etcetera.'

'You tease! I've been thinking about that. It struck me that we don't have to make the bows. All we have to do is cut the ribbon and write Rebecca's name on each one. People can use the strips of ribbon to create their own bows when they tie them on something.'

'So what we did last night was wasted.'

'Never wasted. They were two-hundred prototypes.'

'So that's tonight's job.'

'Yes, unless you have something else in mind.'

'There is something else. We need to make some posters to explain about the bows and invite people to contact us if they know anything.'

'I'd like to have a go at that.'

'I love it when a plan comes together.'

'Me too. We *are* the A Team!'

Saturday 19th May

12

On Saturday morning, while Greg was at the museum, Sally walked down to the village centre with two shoe boxes full of pink ribbons and some posters she had designed and printed. The first call was to The Vicarage.

'She rang the doorbell and the door was answered by Simon. 'Good morning, Sally. What can I do for you.'

'Morning Simon. I was hoping to see Sharon.'

'She's out at the moment. Anything I can do?'

'I phoned Sharon on Thursday evening. I've brought some ribbons for her congregation...'

'... for Rebecca. Sharon told me. Great idea.'

'Here they are.' Sally handed him one of the shoe boxes and some posters. 'The sooner these get out the better.'

Simon smiled. 'If I open the lid, will they escape?'

Amused by the joke, she replied, 'I'm not too sure. You better open the box carefully.'

'That's fine. Leave it with me. By the end of tomorrow they will be all over the place.'

'Thanks.'

'See you soon. Bye.'

Sally's next call was to The Red Lion. It was already open and serving hot drinks. A few people were in the lounge enjoying Terry's freshly ground coffee. He was busy behind the bar as usual.

'Morning Terry. May I ask a favour?'

'You can certainly ask.'

'Greg and I are re-examining Rebecca Stainton's disappearance.'

'Up to your sleuthing again, are you?'

'Well yes. The vicar suggested it. She kind of set it as a challenge.'

'Quite a challenge. It must be three years since.'

'Nearly four-and-a-half actually.'

'Goodness!' He nodded his head while considering it. 'Doesn't time fly? So what can I do?

'You'll remember the pink bows.'

'Yes. All over the place.'

'We've come up with a plan to jog memories. We want to flood the village with some new ribbons. Most of the others have gone.' She lifted the box and removed the lid. 'Would you put this somewhere near the bar so that your customers can take them.' She handed him a poster. 'This explains everything.'

'Of course I will.'

'Thanks. That's so good of you. With a bit of luck, we can get the press interested as well.'

'You were in here last Saturday with some friends, weren't you?'

'Not exactly friends. They were Rebecca's parents

and her brother. Last Saturday was Rebecca's birthday. They'd come to bring some flowers and birthday cards for her at the entrance to The Oaks. I was lucky to meet them and we had lunch together.'

'If I'd known.... Never mind. Okeydoke. I'll sort it. Is Greg alright?'

'Yes. He's at work today.'

'If you fancy another quiz evening, I could organise one.'

'No. Not yet anyway.'

'Understood. Hope to see you both again soon.'

'Thanks. We'll be back, you can be sure.'

Sally crossed the road again and made her way up Smithy Lane to the school entrance. She posted an envelope addressed to *Mrs Young (Headteacher)*, into the letter box attached to the gate. The envelope contained yet another poster, as promised by Greg. From there she doubled back to Church Road and made her way home.

-o0o-

The treasure hunters were spending their third Saturday morning on the towpath with their magnet. On this particular day they decided to try the section at the end of the path that led to the canal from Canal Road.

They took it in turns to throw the magnet and drag it back. After retrieving a broken motorbike chain, a collection of fishing hooks and some large washers, they sat down with cans of beer.

Cliff pondered, 'It would be nice to come up with some gold.'

'Gold isn't magnetic,' Tony blurted scathingly.

'Be that as it may, it would be nice.'

'No chance! Anyway, not many people throw gold away.'

'Rings? You know, like from a spurned lover.'

'Yeah, right! A steel ring with a gold plating no doubt. That would do it.'

'Do you think we'll ever find anything valuable?'

'Depends what you mean by valuable?' Tony replied enigmatically.

'How so?'

'Well, you're assuming a monetary value. There are other sorts of value.' He took a swig from his can before continuing. 'A picture in a metal frame may not have a saleable value, but to the person who knows the subject in the picture it could have sentimental value. A thingamajig might be worthless except to the man who needs it for a particular purpose. To him it has value.'

'Or her,' corrected Cliff.

'Or her.'

'Frankly, I don't much care about sentimental value or, what should we call it, useful value? I just want to find something I can sell, at least to cover the cost of this thing,' he said as he lifted the magnet.

'Is your beer can made of steel or aluminium?'

'How would I know?'

'Is it magnetic?'

'Don't know.' Cliff held his can up to the magnet. It didn't stick. 'No.'

'Then it's aluminium. Drink cans used to be steel. They rust and aren't so good for recycling. Most food cans are still made of steel.'

'I thought they were tin cans.'

'Only tin coated.'

'You learn something every day.' Cliff drained his can and squashed it. 'Time to find something that's valuable, I mean that's worth something. Perhaps some coins. We've already found one.'

'Unlikely. Old coins were made without steel. Apparently, the first 1p and 2p coins made of copper-plated steel weren't minted until the early 1990s. I think it was about 2012 when steel was first used in the making of the silver 5p and 10p coins.'

'So, no valuable coins?'

'Sorry. No.'

Cliff waited before getting up to let a couple pass on their tandem. 'Come on, it's your turn.'

Tony drank the dregs of his beer, laid the can next to the motorbike chain, and took hold of the magnet. 'Here's to nothing,' he said as he hurled the magnet diagonally across the canal. He gave the rope a tug.

'I have something,' he said with a modicum of excitement. Slowly he dragged the object towards him. Cliff leaned over the edge and peered into the murky water. Just before the magnet broke the surface, they gasped as they recognised an ornate candle stick.

'Treasure!' exclaimed Cliff.

'Doubt it,' said Tony pessimistically. 'Can't be gold.

Can't be silver. Can't even be brass. Sorry to disappoint you. It's probably steel with a coating of brass. Of little value.'

'You wait. Cleaned up and put up on eBay, who knows what it'll fetch.' He started to clean it up with his sleeve. 'You'll see.'

'Good luck with that. I'm off. See you again soon.'

Cliff decided to have one more throw. He heard a 'clang' as the magnet struck something. He pulled the magnet in. Attached was a metal flower pot decorated with painted flowers on a sky-blue background. Some of the soil was still inside. *Must have fallen off a narrow boat,* he surmised.

Sunday 20th May

On Sunday morning Greg and Sally drove into Stafford to spend the day with Mark and his family. As their only grandchild, Keily was given a great deal of attention. At nine and a quarter years old, Keily was a 'pretty poppet', a description her 'Gramps' used frequently. Nevertheless, when it was time for the grandparents to return home, they were ready for a rest.

As Sally drove into Whittlebrugh she noticed a pink bow tied to one of the gates of Blakeley Golf Club. She pointed it out to Greg. 'That's new.'

'I wonder if there are any more?'

'Let's drive around and see.'

'Okay, you're in the driving seat. Keep your eyes on your driving. I'll look for the bows.' Sally drove on down Church Road. 'There's one,' exclaimed Greg, 'and another.'

When they reached The Red Lion, they saw a couple tied to the supports of the entrance porch canopy. On the other side of the road, there were half-a-dozen tied to the lychgate, and more on The Vicarage fence. Sally turned the car around at the junction with Burrows Road and Greg pointed out a bow tied to the sign for the Robertses farm shop. Sally turned right into Smithy Road, then left into Honeysuckle Lane and left again into Caulston Road, returning to Church Road and their home at Number 62. On every lamppost a pink bow had been tied.

'I hope all these bows lead to some new information,' said Sally as she switched the engine off.

'So do I.' Greg opened his door. 'After all the time we've spent making bows, it better had.'

They had settled down on their sofa in the lounge with books they were reading, having checked the TV listings and deciding that there was nothing they wanted to watch, when Greg's mobile ringtone sounded. He reluctantly answered only to find it was his sister, Lucy. They didn't call each other very often, so it was a bit of a surprise. Lucy spent a few minutes engaging Greg in general chit-chat about their own families.

'So,' asked Greg, 'what is this really about?'

'Nothing really. I was just remembering Mum and thought I'd give you a call to see how you are.'

'Oh. Okay. I'm alright. The holiday in the Dominican Republic turned out to be a great time. I think Mum would have liked it there, and I think she would have been pleased that she was the one who made it possible for us to go.'

'And you solved a murder as well.'

'More Sally than me, but yes.'

'And you're keeping out of trouble?

'Hardly. We're trying to solve a missing person's cold case. Our former vicar's wife disappeared over four years ago. We've been challenged to find out what happened to her.'

'That sounds exciting.'

'Not sure about that, but we'll do our best.'

'Well, I better go. Give my love to Sally, won't you?'

'Of course. And my best to Pete. Take care. Love you, Sis. Bye.'

'Bye.'

Having related the conversation with his sister to Sally, Greg settled back down to read, although that was not easy as he thought about his mum and his little sister, Lucy, and his big brother, Mike. He hadn't seen either of them since the funeral the previous year and he felt ashamed that he hadn't made more of an effort to meet up. Distance was part of it with Mike in North Wales and Lucy in Bournemouth. Nevertheless, they should make an effort. After all, he reflected, families matter.

Monday 21st May

13

Amy and Chloé were in charge of the sound system in the school hall for the Summer Term in their role as music monitors. For the whole school assembly on this particular Monday morning in May, they had chosen a reflective, instrumental track from one of the CDs in the cupboard. The classes entered and took up their places, the children sitting cross-legged on the floor and the teachers on chairs at the side.

When everyone was ready, Mrs Susan Young moved to the front. She indicated to Amy and Chloé that they should fade out the music and a hush descended on the hall. Susan, along with everyone else present, knew what would happen next. She had experienced the same thing at several schools, but each one was unique in its own way. At her previous school, the children's greeting at the beginning of the whole school assembly was slow and sullen.

When Susan was appointed as Deputy Head at St Philip's, she was relieved that here, the greeting was bright and cheerful. Had she wanted to change it, it would have been very difficult, even as Headteacher because generations of children continued their predecessors' pattern.

'Good morning, everyone.'

'Good morning Mrs Young. Good morning, everybody,' chorused all the children.

'I'm very proud of you all this morning. I can see that you have remembered to sit up straight with your arms folded.' She looked down at the front row where the four and five-year-olds were seated. 'Lucy, you are one of the smartest today. Well done.' Lucy beamed.

'Now, I'd like to ask you a question. Hands up if you have an answer for me.' Two-hundred and seventy young eyes looked up at her expectantly. (Two children were off sick!) 'Have you ever lost anything?'

Hands shot up. 'Leo, what have you lost?'

'I lost my mouse.' Laughter broke out.

'Quiet children.' Then to Leo, 'I'm sorry to hear that. Did you find him?'

'No Miss, Daddy bought me a new one.'

'That's good. Anyone else? Yes Tanya.'

'I lost my Elsa doll.'

'I'm sorry to hear that. Did you find her?'

'Yes Miss, but Bailey had chewed her arm off.'

'Is Bailey your dog?'

'No Miss, he's my baby brother.'

'Oh dear! Tyler, you've had your hand up for a long time, what have you lost?'

'Not me Miss. My dad is always losing his keys. My mum says he's losing his mind as well.'

'Does your dad always find his keys?'

'No Miss, me or Megan find them for him.'

'I remember Megan. She's your big sister isn't she.'

'Yes Miss.'

'One more. Alexis, what have you lost?'

'I've lost my Granddad.'

'I'm sorry to hear that.'

'Don't be sorry Miss. He's gone to be with Granny.'

'Thank you for telling us that, Alexis. Well children, sometimes we lose something or someone and it's really sad. Sometimes we find the things we've lost and we can be happy again. Sometimes we can't find them and then we can be very sad for a long time.'

'This morning I want to tell you about someone who disappeared a few years ago and no one could find her. Her name was Rebecca. Lots of people looked for her. The police looked for her. No one knew where she'd gone. Lots of people are sad and worried about that.'

A hand slowly went up on the back row. 'Ryan. Do you want to say something?'

'Yes Miss. Was that Reverend David's wife?'

'Quite right. Does anyone remember Mrs Stainton?'

Heads turned as children looked around. A few hands went up cautiously at the back of the hall.

'Rebecca Stainton has never been found and some people in Whittlebrugh want to find out what happened to her. They would like *your* help.'

Susan bent down and picked a pink bow out from the cardboard box that Greg had left with her. 'When Rebecca disappeared, pink bows were tied all over our village and nearby, to help people to remember to look for her. Pink was her favourite colour. I have one of these for each of you to take home. We would like you to put your bow where everyone can see it. It could be on your front door, on your gate, in your window.

'If anyone remembers anything that could help us find her, they should tell me, or Reverend Sharon. Your teachers will give out the ribbons at the end of school today with a note to explain to your parents or carers what the ribbon is for.'

A child in the middle of the hall put her hand up confidently. 'Olivia. Do you have a question?'

'Please Miss, what if she's dead?'

'That is possible and very sad. Let's all pray that she is alive.' Susan looked around the hall before continuing. 'Children, in the Bible there is a story Jesus told about something that was missing. Can anyone remember what it was?'

'A sheep.'

'That's right Ryan, but next time remember to put your hand up before answering. It was a sheep. The shepherd had ninety-nine other sheep, but he left them and searched high and low until he found the lost sheep. Then he took the sheep back to the flock. He was so happy that he told his friends and neighbours so they could help him celebrate. Jesus said that no one is lost to God. When someone is lost and then found, everyone can be happy.

'Now children, I'm going to say a prayer and if you want to make the prayer your own, say the 'Amen' at the end.' All the children bowed their heads and many of them closed their eyes and put their hands together.

'Father God, we are sad when we lose people or things. We pray for Rebecca and all who are sad because she hasn't been found. May there be joy instead of sadness, peace instead of worry. We ask this in Jesus' name. Amen.'

The hall was filled with a collective 'Amen'.

- o 0 o -

That evening, pink bows were tied up outside houses all over Whittlebrugh, Caulston and Knowle and a few other places beside.

14

Greg had only just arrived home when his mobile ringtone sounded.

'Hello?'

'Hi. Is that Greg Williams?'

'Who's asking?'

'Oh, sorry. My name's Steve, Steve Jarvis. I saw your name on a poster at The Red Lion last night.'

'Oh, right. What can I do for you?'

'You're interested in finding out what happened to Rebecca Stainton, aren't you?'

'Yes.'

'Have you spoken to Bob White?'

'No. Who's he?'

'Bob lives in Knowle. He's actually a churchwarden there. I remember him telling me about something that happened in Knowle on Boxing Day. It was a week or so before Rebecca went missing. You should talk to him.'

'Can you tell me any more?'

'No. You talk to him.'

The line went dead. *Mysterious.* Greg immediately rang Sharon who gave him Bob's number – a landline. He called it. Bob answered and, after Greg explained the circumstances, invited Greg and Sally to meet him at his home that very evening. So, having had their evening meal, he and Sally made their way to Bob's house.

14 Prospect Terraces was one of twenty-four homes built in a white brick. Each house had a small front garden with a path leading to the front door. Next to the front door of each house, a bay window indicated the position of the front room. Although the twelve houses on each side of the road were terraced, they had been built in pairs, each alternate house being a mirror plan, so the front doors of numbers 14 and 16 were next to each other and they shared a single pitched roof with the gable end facing the road.

Greg opened the gate and took note of the bright pink bow tied to it. An ornate brass knocker was set in the middle of the door. Greg used it in a double hit. Bob opened the door almost immediately.

'Greg, Sally. Nice to meet you. Do come in.' Bob led them into the front room and waved them into Chesterfield style armchairs. 'Can I offer you a drink? Coffee, or something stronger?'

'Coffee would be fine.'

'Excellent. Joan will make them and join us, if that's alright?'

'Perfect,' said Sally. Bob left the room and they looked around. Although the room was dated, it had a comfortable lived-in feeling. There was an open fireplace with hearth and mantelpiece of red brick. In the fire void stood a glass vase of chrysanthemums. The mantelpiece was packed with items including a clock and family photographs.

Two minutes later, Bob and Joan came in with a tray loaded with cups and saucers, plates, serviettes and fairy cakes. Bob held the tray while Joan served.

When they were settled, Bob got down to the purpose of the visit. 'I understand you're looking into Rebecca Stainton's disappearance.'

'We are,' said Greg. 'We don't seem to be getting very far. Steve Jarvis phoned me and told me that we ought to speak to you - something about Boxing Day?'

'Ah yes. Joan and I knew David and Rebecca quite well. As one of the churchwardens at St Saviour's, we met up regularly. We didn't see Rebecca too often, but David was here for the weekly services.'

'Boxing Day?' prompted Sally.

'Hold on a minute. I have something to show you.' He jumped up and opened the doors of a sideboard. He fished about inside and lifted out a shoe box filled with photographs. He sat down again and searched for a few minutes before lifting out half-a-dozen. 'Sorry about that. I'm a bit of a dinosaur. I still like to have my photographs printed.' He selected one. 'This is a picture I took of Rebecca on Boxing Day, not long before she went missing.'

He leaned over and handed it to Sally. They both looked at it. They recognised Rebecca in the centre. She had her hair tied back and was holding a placard. In handwriting, made with a thick pen, it read: *STOP the cruelty. Killing is NOT a sport.*

'Where was this taken?' asked Greg.

'This was on The Green. You can see the horses and

riders of the Knowle Hunt in the background.'

'I've heard about the Boxing Day Hunt,' remarked Sally, 'though I've never seen it.'

'The Hunt goes back for generations. It's a bit of an anachronism now, especially since fox hunting became illegal back in 2004. Its heyday was when Knowle Hall was the centre of the community and Sir Timothy had his own kennels and stables. Nowadays the Boxing Day Hunt continues as a trail hunt. On this particular occasion John Greyson, Sir Andrew's grandson, was there on his own grey. The event still draws anti-hunt campaigners who insist that foxes are still being killed in horrific ways.'

'And Rebecca was one of them?'

'She was *that* year. The thing is, that while the riders were preparing with the traditional sherry, she got into an argy-bargy with one of the riders, Rex Marshall. I saw them shouting at each other and Rebecca was waving that placard as if to unseat him. In retaliation, or perhaps defence, Rex maneuvered his mount so that the rear end pushed her away.'

'Was she hurt?' asked Sally with obvious concern.

'No, but she was mad as hell. After all, no one wants to be at the back end of a horse.' He handed them some more photographs. 'People come from far and wide to watch the spectacle. In those photos you can see locals, visitors and members of the hunt.'

'And this all took place on The Green?'

'It did, as it has done for years. Until it closed in the 1980s, the house on the end of The Green used to be The

Bell Inn. The inn played a major part in the Boxing Day tradition.'

'So,' enquired Greg, 'what do you know about Max?'

'I think you mean Rex. Rex is quite a character. He's very wilful, and a strong supporter of the Hunt, as was his father before him. I don't like to speak ill of the fellow, but I wouldn't want to meet him on a dark night, if you know what I mean.'

Joan scowled at Bob. 'Don't be so melodramatic.'

'Just saying.'

'Is it at all possible,' probed Greg, 'that Rex might have been involved in her disappearance?'

'I really don't know. What I do know is that Rex wasn't even questioned in the aftermath. Well, I don't think so, anyway.'

'And where is he now?'

'Lives with his mother on Forest View. Not that you'll find him there now. I understand he works away during the week as a contractor for a construction company.'

'Thank you. That's given us something to think about. Changing the subject a little... what did you think of David as Vicar?'

'He was okay,' said Joan cautiously. 'He always had time for everyone. He'd stay chatting well after the end of the Wednesday and Sunday services. I'm sure it must have driven Rebecca mad, him being on the last minute for the Whittlebrugh Sunday service every week.'

'And Sharon?'

'She's nice too. We do miss the old traditional things, don't we dear? But I suppose that the church has to move with the times.' Bob remained silent. It was clear that this was a deeply held position. 'We wish the church could be a haven of comfort and stability when everything else is changing.'

Bob took over. 'We have a lovely church and it's my responsibility to make sure that it stays that way. I pride myself in looking after St Saviour's. I have to admit that the congregation is not as large as it used to be, but we're not giving up. The cost of the upkeep would be crippling. However, the Greysons have an ancient, legal responsibility to help maintain the building as it has the family crypt beneath the North Porch. Luckily, the family fulfill their responsibility admirably.'

'Fascinating. Look, we've taken up quite enough of your time.'

'Yes,' added Sally, 'and you have been very generous with your hospitality. Joan, your fairy cakes were absolutely the best.'

'Thank you, Sally. My pleasure indeed. Please come again if you think we can help any more. There'll always be cake.' Her eyes suddenly lit up and she raised her right hand and first finger ready to make a point. 'But not this weekend. Bob and I are away for a few days for the Bank Holiday. We're taking our caravan down to Chetmouth in Devon.'

'That's where I grew up,' said Greg smiling broadly. 'You'll love it. The sea and the surrounding countryside are amazing.'

'We know that. It's probably our favourite place.'

'May we take photos of these photos?' asked Greg as he held up the photographs.

Bob nodded his head. 'Of course.'

Greg pulled out his mobile, laid each photo on the coffee table in turn, and snapped one of each.

They all stood and the Williamses made their way home. They drove around the block, passing St Saviour's Church, The Green and the entrance to Forest View, becoming more familiar with the layout of the village, as they did.

Wednesday 23rd May

15

A phone call on Wednesday morning from the school secretary came in while Greg was at work. 'Mr Williams, would it be possible for you to come into school later this afternoon?'

'I guess,' he said uncertainly.

'Mrs Young thinks you might be interested in something a former pupil has to say regarding Rebecca Stainton.'

'Okay.'

'They can be here at four-thirty. Would that suit you?'

'I can do that.'

'Excellent. I'll let Mrs Young know. Goodbye.'

Intriguing.

- o 0 o -

As Greg walked down to the school, he was astonished by the number of pink bows all over the place. Hundreds of them had appeared. He recognised the style and material of many as those that he and Sally had made. Others, however, were made from other materials and tied in different ways. All of them bore Rebecca's name. Clearly

95

the idea had taken root. He arrived at the end of Smithy Road, turned the corner, and was accosted by Mrs Talbot. Even though the weather was very pleasant, she was wearing her hat. Greg was wary of her as she had the reputation of being the village gossip.

'Good afternoon Mr Williams.'

'Good afternoon Mrs Talbot.'

'I hear you and Mrs Williams are looking into the mystery of the old Vicar's wife... not that she was old.'

'You've heard correctly.'

'So, you hope to solve another mystery then?'

'We would certainly like to.'

'Well, if I hear anything I would be happy to share it with you.'

'That's very kind.'

'Not at all. Always have my ear to the ground. Have you any new leads?'

'Sorry, not really. Do excuse me. I have an appointment.'

'Have you?' It was obvious that she would have liked to know more.

'See you around. Bye.' He moved around her and carried on down the road towards the school.

The car park was still full. He approached the pedestrian gate and pressed the intercom button.

'Hello. How may I help?'

'Mr Williams to see Mrs Young.'

'Good afternoon. Please pull the gate open and close it behind you.' There was a buzzing noise and Greg opened and closed the gate as instructed. He strode up the path and was met by the school secretary who was holding the door open for him. 'Welcome to St Philip's School. Come in.'

He followed her to the office. 'I'll get you signed in and give you a visitor's badge. School has finished, but regulations... you know.'

When the formalities were completed, she led him to the Head's room, tapped on the door and opened it. 'Mr Williams to see you.'

'Come in Greg.' Susan was sitting behind her desk. There was one empty chair. Three other chairs were already occupied. 'May I introduce you to Mrs Groves and her sons, Ryan and Brandon.' Hellos were said all round. Greg sat in the empty chair. 'I've asked you to come because Brandon here,' she indicated the older boy, 'has something to say. It may be significant to your enquiries.'

Brandon's mother stepped in. 'When Ryan came home on Monday with the pink bow, we thought little of it until Brandon arrived from his school.'

Susan interrupted. 'Brandon attended St Philip's before he moved up to Stafford Court Academy three years ago.'

'That's right. Anyway,' Mrs Groves continued, 'Brandon told us about something I had forgotten all about - something that he saw on the day Mrs Stainton disappeared. We didn't think anything of it at the time. After all, eleven-year-old boys have extraordinary imaginations, don't they?'

'How about we let Brandon tell us?' suggested Susan.

His mother nodded permission.

'I remember it really well. Grandad collected me and Ryan from school as usual and took us to his house on Meadowside. His house is right at the end. It was cold so we went to their spare bedroom to play.

'Anyway, we heard a noise outside so we looked out of the window. We can see the road that goes to Knowle from there. On the other side of the road is a layby. People park there when they want to go onto the towpath. There was a big car there and we saw Mrs Stainton getting out of the car.

'Then a man got out of the driver's side. He rushed around the car and it looked like he was arguing with her. He opened the door, she got back in. He shut the door and rushed back around to his door, got in and drove off over the canal bridge.'

Greg was excited, but had questions. 'How did you know it Mrs Stainton?'

'She was wearing a long dark coat, but we recognised her. Grandad and Gran used to take us to church, so we knew her from there.'

'Did you recognise the man?'

'No. He had a coat and a hat. We never got to see his face.'

'Did you tell anyone?'

'Not straight away. It was the next day. We went to Grandad and Gran's house as usual. Then, when we went home, Dad was talking about her being missing. That's when we told Mum and Dad what we'd seen. They didn't believe us.'

Mrs Groves explained. 'You have to remember that Brandon was only eleven and Ryan was just seven. It seemed a far-fetched story. More than that, I don't really remember too much about it all, except that my husband joined in the search for Rebecca and he came back freezing cold.'

'I did the same,' remarked Greg. 'So Brandon, you think you saw Mrs Stainton...'

'...we *did* see her,' insisted Ryan. 'Don't you believe us?' He was riled and almost in tears.

Susan took over. 'I'm sure you're telling the truth, both of you. It's a shame you weren't able to tell your story back then. Perhaps things might have turned out differently. I'm pleased you've had the opportunity now and I'm proud of you for that. However, I'd just like to get this straight. You had gone home with your grandad from school. You had been there some time. It was the middle of January. Wasn't it too dark to see anything properly?'

'No,' Brandon said defiantly. 'It was *still* light.'

Susan tapped on her computer keyboard and read from the screen. 'January fifteenth. Sunset is four-twenty. There would still be some light until about four-forty.'

'Is there anything else you can tell us?' asked Greg.

'I don't think so.' Brandon looked at his brother.

Ryan shook his head then asked, 'Do you think you'll be able to find her?'

'We're going to do our very best. Thank you. You have been a big help. And thank you, Mrs Groves for bringing your boys in.'

'Well,' said Susan, standing up, 'that seems to be that. Nice to see you again Brandon. See you tomorrow, Ryan.' She opened the door and passed them over to the secretary to return their badges and let them out. Greg parted company with the boys and their mother at the school gate. He ambled home pondering what he had just heard. *Who was the man in the big car?*

A couple of men passed him. One of them was holding a length of rope with a round cylinder attached. *What on earth....*

16

Cliff was determined to have another go. In fact, he was becoming obsessed with his new hobby. He had convinced himself that there was treasure to be found and that he would find it if he spent enough time searching the muddy waters of the canal. He took comfort from the fact that he had already found several items. He was sure that if he had gone for a metal detector, he wouldn't have found anything in the short time that he had been active with the magnet.

Tony, on the other hand, was skeptical. He was willing to go along with Cliff's quest, but was equally sure that it was a mug's game. Only rubbish was thrown away. They had been friends since they were at primary school and the friendship was more valuable than wasting a few hours with a fishing magnet.

On this outing, Cliff had decided to return to the bridge on Knowle Lane having considered the likelihood that treasure was more likely to be thrown from a bridge than a towpath in the middle of nowhere. So, it was back there that they were heading.

It was a very pleasant May afternoon, so much so that they were both wearing Tshirts and shorts. As they walked along Knowle Lane they could see the bright yellow of the rapeseed crop in the fields around them and even the pungent smell was caught on the gentle breeze.

They left the road just after the layby, taking the steps down onto the towpath.

'Here we go,' Cliff said hopefully as he tossed the magnet into the water on the far side of the canal. He dragged it back. There was nothing attached. Straight away he had a second go. 'Nothing again. You have a go.'

Tony took the magnet and dropped it close to the side, walking along the towpath, dragging the magnet along as he walked. After about twenty metres, he stopped and lifted it out. 'Third time lucky,' he said as he proudly exhibited a rusty, twenty-centimeter long, cold chisel.

'Show off!' Cliff took the magnet away from his friend and walked back to the bridge. He waited while a motor cruiser passed. Just to be different, he lobbed the magnet under the road bridge, but expected little. When he began to pull it back in, he knew he had caught something and his anticipation leapt.

'Quick. Come here. I've got something.' He could feel the drag of the object across the bottom of the canal through the tension of the rope. As it broke the surface he could see a cylinder about half-a-metre long. He lifted it onto the path and expressed his disappointment. 'Oh well, just an old fire extinguisher.'

Tony examined it and then said in a forceful tone, 'Cliff, for the love of God, don't touch it.'

'What's wrong mate?'

'Just leave it where it is and come with me.'

'Why?'

'That's no fire extinguisher.'

-o0o-

Greg busied himself preparing the evening meal for when Sally would arrive home as was the norm for a Wednesday. It was almost ready when he heard the sound of a siren going past. A few minutes later there was another one. He decided to step into the garden to have a look and was turning to go back inside when he heard another siren approaching. It grew louder until a police van passed at speed and the tone of the siren changed as it sped towards the centre of the village.

'Hi Greg.' Sally had slipped in and was standing in the kitchen as he re-entered with their dog racing ahead of him to greet her mistress. 'What's all that about?' she asked.

'No idea. Must be something big. That's the third siren I've heard going by.'

'I'll check Facebook,' she said pulling out her mobile. She perched on a stool and navigated into the Whittlebrugh Community page. Nothing significant had been posted, so she posted a question hoping that someone would know something.

They were half way through eating their meal when a notification 'ping' sounded. She read the text out loud.

Not sure whats happening but police have closed Knowle Lane to vehicles and pedestrians

'Goodness! Perhaps there's been an accident,' suggested Greg. Almost immediately there was another 'ping'.

Meadowside ppl are being evacuated

'More than an accident.'

'Do you think it might be a gas leak?'

'Who knows?'

'ping'

Meadowside residents being taken to Church Hall

'Yeah. A gas leak.

'ping'

Bomb found in canal. Bomb squad being called in

-oOo-

Cliff had taken a more careful look at the cylinder. It was only then that he noticed the fins. Tony had told him that it was probably a mortar bomb. They left it where it was and returned to their cars. Tony had called 9 9 9. He thought the person on the other end sounded a little skeptical at first, but had assured him that officers had been dispatched to the site.

Eight and a half minutes later he had heard the first siren approaching, then a second. The officers asked them a few questions and then walked onto the bridge and looked down to see the object lying on the towpath with the magnet still attached. There was some chatter on the radios. The second police car to arrive was driven over the bridge towards Knowle for a couple of hundred yards, where it blocked the road.

Cliff and Tony were instructed to return to Church Road. A police van arrived and the officers set about evacuating the residents from near-by homes, including everyone in Meadowside.

Within thirty minutes of Tony's call, a bomb squad based at the Stafford Barracks where Sally worked, arrived on site. By then there was an even greater police presence including a Staffordshire Police Force *Major Incident Command and Control* vehicle'.

-o0o-

'How about we take a stroll down to The Red Lion,' suggested Greg nonchalantly.

'It's a very nice evening for a walk,' said Sally, keeping up the pretence. 'I know Debbie would appreciate stretching her legs.'

Greg cleared the table hastily. 'Come on. Let's go.'

Within a minute they were walking towards the scene. Blue lights were flashing and, even from a distance, they could see a crowd of people gathered in the area between the lychgate and the pub.

They reached the scene and mingled with the crowd to try to find out what they could about the bomb. There was not much information circulating until two men came out of the police's *Major Incident Command and Control* vehicle. They were recounting their part in the drama when the first of a battery of journalists arrived from local radio stations and newspapers. Reporters with microphones jostled their way through the crowd in pursuit of newsworthy comments and pictures.

Someone told Greg that the men being interviewed were locals called Cliff and Tony. Apparently, they had been magnet fishing in the canal and had found a World

War Two unexploded bomb.

When the frenzy died down, a journalist approached Greg. 'Hi, my name's Graham Tetley from Stafford Mail. I noticed pink ribbons all over the place. A lady in a hat told me that you were the person to speak to about them. Is that right?'

'Actually, yes. I'm Greg Williams and this is my wife, Sally. We're trying to find out about Rebecca Stainton who disappeared more than four years ago.'

'Oh yes. I remember that. She was the vicar's wife, if my memory serves me right.

'Quite right. Our present vicar challenged us to delve into the mystery. The trouble is that most people have forgotten about it.'

'Or even if they haven't forgotten,' added Sally, 'there has been no one probing what is now a 'cold case'.'

Graham had started scribbling notes on a pad. 'So, do you think you can crack the case when detectives gave up?'

Sally drew a breath then responded. '*We* think that it's better to be asking questions than not.'

'And,' added Greg, 'with our local knowledge, it might just be possible.'

'So what's with the ribbons?'

'If you covered the story before, you should surely remember the pink ribbons that were tied here and there around the village. These new ones are a way of reminding people. We hope that some new information will surface.'

'And has it?'

Greg looked at Sally to answer. She did so cautiously.

'We're following up something that *might* lead us somewhere, but for now we'd like to keep it to ourselves.'

'Can you give me something?'

Greg took a more discreet tone. 'Look, we would like to tell you more, but we don't want to raise hopes and then have them dashed. Rebecca still has family and friends who are anxious to have news. So, if you don't mind, we would like to keep what we have to ourselves. Having said that, we would be happy for you to report what we are doing and invite anyone who has any new information to get in touch.'

'I think I can do something. I'll have a chat to my editor. I have a photographer here. Could I get a picture of you two, perhaps with pink bows in the shot, for our paper and online version?'

They agreed. Graham wrote a few more details down before calling his colleague over. The young woman photographer took them across the road to the lychgate. Several pink bows were tied to it. They tied Debbie up to a nearby lamppost. The photographer didn't take long and they turned to leave for home.

'Are you famous now?' asked Sharon from behind.

Greg turned towards her. 'Hello Sharon. Not yet. It's all in a good cause, though. A journalist from Stafford Mail wanted to know about the pink bows. I think we may land the publicity we were looking for.'

'Well done,' she replied admiringly. 'Sorry, I must fly. I'm organising accommodation, food and drinks in the Church Hall for some temporarily homeless souls. Take care. Bye.'

- o 0 o -

In the News Room at Stafford Mail, Graham's first job was to write up his piece on the Whittlebrugh bomb discovery for the printed version to be published on Friday. He then adapted it for the online version which would be uploaded immediately the editor had checked it.

Next, he turned to the story of the missing woman. He looked up the articles from January four years previous. He reminded himself of the details before knocking on the editor's door. The next few minutes were spent arguing the benefits of re-visiting the story after so much time. He was able to show him the photographs of Greg and Sally and emphasise the personal element of their challenge. He left the office with a big smile on his face.

Before he left for home, he completed his initial article regarding Rebecca's disappearance and the hope of solving the mystery at last. Like his previous copy, it would be checked by the editor before being uploaded to the online edition. He made a mental note to try and contact Rebecca's husband and family. Once out of the office, he would put it out of his mind and enjoy his home time as he had taught himself to do over many years.

Thursday 24th May

17

When the 7am alarm sounded on his clock, Graham sat up and listened to the local radio news. It informed him that the Army's Explosive Ordnance Disposal Regiment Team were to detonate the Whittlebrugh bomb at 10am. That gave him plenty of time to make his way there and see it for himself.

He arrived in the village soon after 9am. The police had made a cordon with a special area set aside for reporters in a field off Burrows Road normally used for grazing sheep. What he hadn't quite bargained for, was the interest from national press and media. He recognised some of the others including Ed from Reuters and a reporter from local radio, but couldn't remember her name. The symbols on the TV vans spoke for themselves.

A diversion had been set up via Burrows Road for people wanting to get to Knowle. It would add on another four miles to the journey.

From the press and media designated area they could see the field of rapeseed beyond the canal. A track had been laid down overnight from the canal bridge to the centre of the field, allowing a mechanical digger to excavate a hole. They had been careful to minimalise damage to the crop.

At a-quarter-to-ten, an Army officer with the rank of Captain gave a press conference during which time he explained what was going to happen. He explained that the mortar had been buried in the field and that Cliff Johnson, the man who had retrieved the bomb from the floor of the canal, would be given the privilege of pressing the button to detonate the explosion.

Graham managed to get in a question regarding the safety of the public. The captain gave an assurance that no one would be harmed as long as they were outside the cordon. He then excused himself so that he could get on with his duties.

At precisely 10am, just as the chimes of the clock on St Philip's Church rang out, an explosion was heard, a vibration was felt, and an eruption of soil could be seen from the rapeseed field. A cheer was heard from the crowd of people gathered in the car park of the Red Lion and in the churchyard. Soon afterwards, the reporters and the local people began to disperse.

Ed from Reuters moseyed over to Graham. 'Saw your piece online about the missing woman. Rebecca, wasn't it?'

'Oh! Right. Seems like the story may have life in it again, though whether Rebecca is still alive is less probable.'

'And that's what all these pink bows are about?'

'Apparently.'

'Anything else I should know.'

'Not really. Nothing as yet. I might keep an eye on it, but I can't see it coming to anything – just a couple of locals trying to solve the mystery. Can't see how they can find anything when so much time has passed and when the police did a thorough job back then.'

'In other words, if there's a scoop to be had, you'll keep it to yourself. I get it. Just remember who your friends are, Graham.'

'Okay, Ed. I tell you what, if I hear there's a break in the case, I'll tip you off. Fair enough? After all, that's what friends are for!'

'That's my man. Better go now. Have to get this one in.'

Graham watched him walk away towards the pub. *I wonder if he can let it go so easily?* He followed shortly afterwards.

At the junction of Knowle Lane with Church Road, the police were in the process of removing the cordon and opening the lane back up to vehicles and pedestrians. Residents of the lane and Meadowside were walking back to their homes. They looked tired and were walking wearily.

Coming the other way, he saw Cliff Johnson whom he had seen the day before. He decided to have a chat with him about his experience. He was over the moon and very happy to talk about what happened, about pulling up the cylinder, realising it was a bomb, phoning the police, meeting the Bomb Squad, pressing the button. Once started, it was hard to stop him. 'Will I be in the paper?' he asked.

'I'll make sure of it.'

'Thanks,' he said, as he all but skipped away.

Friday 25th May

18

WWII BOMB BLAST

In the sleepy village of Whittlebrugh near Stafford, an unexploded World War 2 bomb, which had been found by a local man who had been magnet fishing in the canal, was safely detonated this morning by the Army Explosive Ordnance Disposal Regiment Team (Bomb Squad). Mr Cliff Johnson, a local resident, who fished the mortar bomb out, was given the privilege of pressing the button...

...Whittlebrugh was in the news four-and-a-half years ago when Rebecca Stainton, the vicar's wife, went missing. Local people and the police searched for her, but to no avail. Local amateur sleuths, Greg and Sally Williams have recently set about solving the mystery and are hopeful of bringing resolution for Rebecca's husband and family. If anyone has...

Greg's phone began ringing and buzzing soon after the news report was published on the Stafford Mail's online news page. The calls and messages came in from various print and broadcast organisations. After the first two, and as he was still at work, he let them all go to voicemail.

In the middle of the afternoon he messaged Sally and discovered that she, too, had been getting similar attention. Neither of them knew how their mobile numbers had been discovered so quickly by so many reporters. They agreed to talk about it when they arrived home after work. Nevertheless, both of them found it hard to concentrate on the job in hand.

By the time they sat down together in the kitchen, Sally had decided that Greg should be the spokesperson. They made a joint list of the people who had contacted them and decided to return the calls or messages in the order they received them. There were fifteen in all.

Then they wrote down what they thought were the salient points they wanted to get across. Greg was nervous when he began at the top of the list. However, as the conversations and questions continued, he became more confident, especially as Sally was there to prompt him. Some messages just required an invitation to call him back out of office hours.

When he had completed, all fifteen he felt drained and hungry. So the evening meal, defrosted from the freezer, was very welcome.

While they were washing up Sally asked, 'Do you realise that next Monday is a Bank Holiday?'

'It is. I'm looking forward to having a rest.'

'I have another idea – a far better one.'

'Right?' Greg said warily, not hiding his concern for her *far better one*.

'I thought we might go away for the weekend.'

'And...'

'And we could visit somewhere we've never been before.'

'Like...'

'Like the Yorkshire Dales.'

'*If* we were to go away, do you honestly think we could find somewhere to stay over Spring Bank Holiday Weekend with such little notice? It's bound to be full.'

'But it's not.'

'So you've already checked?'

'Just a peek.'

'And you've found somewhere.'

'A B&B in the village of Totterington, just north of Cargrave.'

'Wherever that is.'

'It's a beautiful area, part of the Yorkshire Dales National Park. It's only just over two hours away. Even if you can't take tomorrow off, we could still be up there in time for supper and return on Monday evening ready for work on Tuesday. What do you say?'

'Do I have a choice?'

'Not really. I've already booked! But you'll love it.'

'I'm sure I will.' He thought for a moment and came up with a question. 'Am I missing something?'

'No. Not really... except for the teeny-weeny bit of information that might explain everything.'

'Okay. Let's hear it.'

'Well, Totterington and the neighbouring village of Smallbridge share the same vicar, a man called David Stainton.'

'So, it's not really a restful couple of days in The Dales, but a chance to further our investigations.'

'True, but in my defence, we should be able to see

some lovely countryside as well.'

'Have you packed the bags yet?' he asked sarcastically.

'Not yet. But it won't take long.

-o0o-

It was soon after 9pm when Greg and Sally received a phone call they didn't expect. It was from Robert Stainton. He called Sally because he had seen a news item on TV about the Whittlebrugh Bomb with a mention of Rebecca's disappearance. He wanted to know if they had made any headway in their investigations. Sally told him that there were a few things they were looking into, but that there was nothing concrete. She told him about the new pink ribbons and their planned trip to Yorkshire with the hope of 'bumping' into David. Robert said he might be able to smooth their way. She promised to let him know if they discovered anything new and significant in their quest, and finished the call.

Saturday 26th May

At 4pm Sally met Greg at the Museum having first dropped off Debbie at Mark and Rosie's house, in the knowledge that their granddaughter, Keily, would be thrilled to look after her for a couple of days. She left her car in the museum car park and they transferred into his Dacia Duster.

She drove the first part of the journey north. The

traffic around Manchester was heavy and slowed them down. Greg took over once they left the motorway. They arrived at their accommodation at ten-past seven. The house was built of stone with a small glazed porch in the centre. There was a sash window on each side and two on the first floor. Mrs Rawlinson welcomed them with a smile and the delightful news that their supper, a casserole, was ready to be served. They took the bags Sally had packed that morning, up to their room, before returning downstairs.

As Mrs Rawlinson served up their meal in the dining room, situated to the right of the central hallway, she explained that there was another lady staying in the bedroom across the landing from theirs.

'She comes here quite often,' she explained. 'She sometimes brings her teenage son with her, but not this weekend. She's very sweet. I think her husband died, or perhaps they just separated. You'll probably bump into her at some point.'

Sally and Greg devoured their meal and topped it off by accepting the offer of a hot chocolate 'with all the extras'.

They made their way back up to their room and took a good look around. The room was pleasant, though the flowery wallpaper was not one the Williamses would have chosen – a bit chintzy for their liking. The most important thing was that the bed was extremely comfortable.

Sally checked that their car was okay before drawing the curtains. As she did so, she noticed a bright orange VW

Golf being parked behind their white Dacia Duster. A young woman stepped out and locked the door. Sally couldn't see much because of the angle from the bedroom window. What she could see clearly as the woman stepped into the light from the front door, was that her hair was red – the colour of red wine.

Lying awake in bed, Sally began to regret her decision to make the trip north. In the stillness of the night it seemed to be a foolish escapade. There was a chance David would not want to be tracked down; would not want to talk about Rebecca; would not want to delve into the past. *Wasn't this all a bit impertinent of them? Who were they to think they could solve the mystery.*

The doubts went round and round in her head and robbed her of sleep. She tried to distract herself by thinking of other things, but thoughts of David's potential reaction to their presence soon returned.

She took a peek at the bedside digital clock radio. It was one-fifty-two. She began counting sheep for the umpteenth time and eventually drifted off.

Sunday 27th May

19

Sunday morning came all too soon. Greg had enjoyed a deep sleep. Sally had slept well once she had nodded off. Neither were anxious to leave the comfort of the deep mattress. They had agreed to have breakfast at nine o'clock and were far too polite to be late for their host. The mantelpiece clock had just finished striking nine when they entered the dining room. On offer was a full English breakfast or fruit and cereals. They opted for the Full English.

While they waited, they enjoyed a glass of fruit juice and looked out of the window. Across the road they could see a few houses built in a similar style to the one in which they were staying. Each had a small front garden accessed by a gate recessed into a stone wall. The garden flowers were blooming in a magnificent display of colours. The sky, meanwhile, looked grey and threatening.

Their cooked breakfast arrived and Mrs Rawlinson placed a pot of fresh coffee on the side table with a jug of milk. They tucked into their breakfast as if they hadn't eaten for days. The other guest entered and they watched, surreptitiously, as she served herself a bowl of cereal from the side table before sitting at a small table by the window.

Sally attempted a conversation. 'Hello. The weather doesn't look very promising, does it?'

'No.'

'This is our first time to The Dales. You've been before, haven't you?'

'Yes, a few times.'

'We're thinking of having a look around. Where would you recommend?'

'You'd better ask Yvonne, Mrs Rawlinson. She's bound to know.'

'I'll do that. Thank you.' Clearly this guest was not in the chatting mood.

They finished off their breakfast with some fresh toast and some delicious homemade marmalade.

Sally's plan was to meet up with David. She had discovered that he would be taking the service at the Totterington Parish Church at nine-thirty, and at Smallbridge at eleven o'clock. They had already missed the start of the service at the local church, so they prepared to drive the few miles to Smallbridge. The rain started and continued to fall steadily. They were relieved to have brought their waterproof coats. They ran all the way from their car to the church porch with their hoods pulled up.

The church was small with a simple nave and chancel. A pulpit was tucked into the corner of the nave in front of the chancel arch. A brass eagle lectern occupied the space opposite. The pews were upright and they felt uncomfortable straight away. Sally leaned over and whispered in Greg's ear. 'Should have brought cushions.

Perhaps that's why there aren't many in the congregation.'

There were only eight other people present, excluding David and the organist. It made both of them feel conspicuous. David entered in his robes and the service began. Luckily neither the service nor the sermon went on for long. David appeared to look directly at them quite often. It made them feel quite self-conscious.

At the end, David made his way to the door. When they shuffled out with the others, he spoke to them warmly. 'Good morning. Sally and Greg isn't it? Robert phoned me and told me you might be coming.' He stretched out his hand to shake theirs. 'I couldn't put faces to names until I saw you, then I recognised you. I don't know what you might have planned. Would you like to come for some supper, just a few nibbles, at The Rectory in Totterington? I'd like to hear what's happening in my old patch. A World War Two bomb, according to the news.'

'Thank you. That would be nice,' said Sally enthusiastically and relieved after her anxiety of the night.

'Excellent. My six o'clock service finishes at around seven, so... let's say seven-thirty.'

'Seven-thirty it is.'

'Thank you,' added Greg. 'See you then.'

The rain was continuing as they returned to the car. They decided to inform Mrs Rawlinson about their plans and ask her where they should do some 'sightseeing'.

Back at the B&B they told Mrs Rawlinson that they had been invited to The Rectory by David Stainton, so they would be out until later in the evening. She suggested they should try the pub in the village for lunch and, weather permitting, visit Malham Cove.

The pub was quite full, though the landlord did find them a table where they enjoyed a drink and succumbed to the temptations of the advertised Sunday Roast.

It took them twenty minutes to drive to Malham village where they found an unexpectedly large car park. It was already quite full. Fortunately, the rain had paused. At an information centre they bought a map and guide. It was apparent that this was a very popular place for walking. The paths were made of crushed white stone. Some walkers, like them, were obviously out for a stroll. Others were dressed and equipped for a long-distance hike.

They weren't sure what to expect as their only understanding of a cove was at the coast where the sea came into a small beach. When they saw what was in front of them, they were amazed. The cove, according to the guide, *'is a white curved cliff, eighty metres high and three-hundred metres wide. A river flows from the bottom of the cliff having passed along a meandering route within the limestone rock.'*

It was magnificent. They decided to climb the four-hundred steps to the top. The climb was breathtaking in more ways than one. The views were spectacular. Down below they could see the people walking to the base of the cliff and the river as it gushed from the rock. From their advantage point, the people down below looked like ants making their way to and from a source of food. Sheep wandered around while Spring lambs could be seen frolicking in the nearby fields. Greg and Sally agreed that the trip to Yorkshire was worth it just for this.

'It's lovely, isn't it?' They were somewhat startled to discover that David was standing behind them. 'I love to come here. I find it so inspiring. I'm reminded of verses from the Bible such as Psalm ninety-five: *In his hand are the depths of the earth, and the mountain peaks belong to him. The sea is his, for he made it, and his hands formed dry land.*'

Sally, having glanced around, returned to take in the view. 'You're very lucky to live and work in such an amazing place.'

'You have no idea. However, I have a service to take soon, so I better dash. See you later.'

'By the way, while I remember,' said Sally, 'I promised Jack Taylor that I'd pass on his regards.'

'Good old Jack. How is he?'

'Not so well.'

'I'm sorry to hear that. Well, bye for now.' And off he strode.

As they made their way down the steps the rain started again. Consequently, their decent was a little dicey. When they arrived back on level ground they hurried back through the village to the car park.

'Isn't that the woman from the B&B,' observed Sally and pointed, 'the one with the red hair getting into that orange Golf?'

'Isn't that David getting in the passenger seat?' asked Greg in disbelief.

'Well, I'll be....'

20

The mystery woman wasn't at the B&B when they arrived back there. Mrs Rawlinson offered them a hot drink which they accepted happily. She also gave them directions to The Rectory - a short walk away.

Unfortunately, it was raining again when it was time to go, so they wore their waterproof coats. They found The Rectory easily by following their host's directions. It was a large, rambling house. The walls were covered with climbing roses in bud. They guessed that the roses would probably look stunning in a few weeks. A wisteria, surrounding the front door, was already blossoming.

David had the door open even before they had reached it. He welcomed them in and led them to the Drawing Room.

The 'nibbles' he promised were laid out on a sideboard and were much more substantial than they had expected. Sally wondered how he had managed to prepare everything at short notice knowing that he had been at Malham in the afternoon and had just returned from taking his evening service.

She and Greg were invited to sit on one of two well-used, comfortable sofas. In front of them, set into a wide chimney breast, was a generous fireplace. In one of the alcoves hung a large screen television. To the left they had a view of the driveway and shrubs through a bay window. She had already noticed that, against the back wall behind them, stood an upright piano. The fallboard was open and the music stand held a hymn book. On the top was a wedding photograph of David and Rebecca.

The most unusual and unexpected items in the room were in the second alcove - life size cut-outs of Luke Skywalker and Princess Leia!

'Do you like them?' asked David. 'I'm really into Star Wars. I'm sometimes tempted to end a service with *May the force be with you.* I haven't had the courage yet.'

'I love 'em,' said Greg with a beaming face. 'In fact, I'm quite jealous.'

'Thanks. They do startle some of my parishioners when they first come in. Now, please come and help yourselves before the food gets hot!'

They were relieved that they had chosen not to eat at the B&B. They filled their plates with samples of all the 'nibbles'. These included delicate finger sandwiches, cheese and crackers, cocktail sausages, and sliced fruit. While they piled their plates, David offered and poured wine into crystal glasses.

They returned to their seats. Near them, their host had placed small wooden tables drawn from a nest.

David filled his own plate and then began asking them about Whittlebrugh. He wanted to know about the bomb, The Oaks Nursing Home, St Phillip's School, and some of the people especially Philip, his old churchwarden and friend, and his wife, Patricia. It was noticeable that he did not ask about the church and the new vicar.

'Robert says that you're trying to find out what happened to Rebecca. It's something I've been waiting to find out for well over four years. Every day I wonder...' He drew a deep breath. 'You can't imagine what it feels like.'

'You're right,' said Sally compassionately. 'I really can't imagine. Sharon, our new vicar, thought we might have a chance by talking to people in the area.'

'Do *you* think you have a chance?'

'Actually,' said Greg, putting his plate down, 'I think we have at least as much chance now as the police had at the time. We've already found some new information.'

David was stunned. 'Really?'

Sally didn't want to raise his hopes too high. 'Well, it may be something or nothing. It came from two young boys who think they saw Rebecca getting into a *big* car. The car was driven away by a man towards Knowle.'

'Where was this?' David demanded.

'The layby near the canal on Knowle Lane.'

'When?'

'The afternoon she disappeared. The boys told us that they were watching from an upstairs window of their grandparent's home in Meadowside.'

David closed his eyes and rubbed his temple. He suddenly looked up. 'Would that be Brandon Groves?'

They were shocked. 'You remember him?' asked Greg.

'Only just. Mr and Mrs Groves brought the boys to church quite often. Rebecca taught in the Sunday School so they would have recognised her for sure. Now, what was his little brother's name? Umm, Brian?'

'Ryan.'

'Yes. Ryan. But he was only a youngster – only about five.'

'Six actually. They told their parents what they saw at the time, but their story was ignored as it was considered as vivid imagination. Neither of them completely forgot what they saw. When Ryan went home from school the other day with a pink bow bearing Rebecca's name, Brandon retold their story and this time his parents decided to pass it on.'

'Wow. Who was this man?'

'We've no idea,' began Sally, 'but it's something the police wouldn't have known. It's the only new information we've found as yet. That's why we're here. We visited Philip and Patricia the other day. They told us that you had allowed them to read Rebecca's diary. I was wondering... I don't want to put you under any pressure, or bring up feelings you would rather not revisit, but might it be possible...'

David had closed his eyes once more. They left him to his thoughts. Greg and Sally looked at each other, not knowing what to say. In the silence they took a sip from their wine glasses.

At last, without opening his eyes, David asked, 'What do you think you might find?'

'I really don't know. Maybe something that only a woman would be able to see in what she wrote.'

'Patricia didn't find anything.' He looked straight at Sally.

'I might not, but *I* think it's worth a try.' She went on to explain her thinking. 'We have to return home tomorrow. If I could borrow Rebecca's diary for just a few hours, then there's a chance I might find a clue. Who knows? I promise that it'll be back in your hands tomorrow before we leave. Please David.'

He pondered it for a few long moments, took a mouthful of wine and then stood up and left the room.

'Do you think we've gone too far?' she asked Greg.

'Not sure.' The room was silent except for the ticking of a clock somewhere out in the hallway.

David returned carrying a wooden box. He sat down and held it tenderly on his knees. It was quite obvious that the box was very precious to him. The box itself was made of a red wood - perhaps mahogany - and was finely crafted with brass fittings. He turned the key and opened the lid. From where they were sitting, they couldn't see what was inside, but they realised there must have been a few items as David appeared to delve down into it.

He withdrew a book. 'This is Rebecca's last diary. I've never read this myself,' he admitted. 'Others have, including the detectives. *If* I loan it to you, will you promise faithfully that you will not disclose anything that would bring embarrassment to me or her family, or, for that matter, damage *her* reputation?'

'I promise on my heart,' said Sally as she lifted her hand to her chest.

He closed the box, placed it on the floor beside his seat, stood up and gave the book to Sally. 'I want it back here tomorrow. Right?'

'Of course. As promised.'

The solemnity of the moment was broken by Greg. 'We really enjoyed visiting Malham Cove this afternoon. Do you go there often?'

David retook his seat. 'Not often enough.'

'It's quite a wonder.'

'It is. There are so many lovely places around here. I'm so lucky to live here. It's so very calming. Mind you, in winter it can be terribly isolated. A good fall of snow and we can be stranded for days, perhaps even weeks. Always good to have the freezer stocked up.'

'We're staying with Mrs Rawlinson, you know. Your friend is staying there too.'

'Oh! Ummm. You've met Vanessa.'

Sally saw his embarrassment. 'She's very nice.'

'She is,' confirmed David. 'Long story. We were at school together. Met up after Rebecca disappeared. She was already divorced. We've become good friends - no more I assure you, I'm a clergyman after all.'

'No need to explain,' Sally insisted, though now feeling embarrassed herself. 'It's none of our business anyhow.' She elbowed Greg and stood up. 'David, you've been very hospitable. Thank you so much for this evening. I think it's time for us to leave, after all,' she held up the diary, 'I have some reading to do.'

David stood. 'I'll see you tomorrow. Take care of it won't you?'

'I certainly will. Don't be worried.'

They hastened out of The Rectory and walked back to their digs. Sally clutched Rebecca's diary under her coat.

Greg smirked. 'Vanessa! A good friend!'

'Stop it, Greg. As I said, it's none of our business.'

21

Greg and Sally climbed into bed. Sally pulled her pillows up to the headboard, so that she could sit up comfortably. She held Rebecca's diary carefully. The book's original cover had been hand covered with white paper on which an artist had painted pictures of wild flowers. The spine had brown gum paper down its length to give it strength and the corners had triangles of the same material. In the centre of the front, in a calligraphy flourish, were the words *Dear Diary*.

Greg turned his bedside lamp off and settled down. Sally opened the diary and noted that, after a couple of blank pages, the first entry was dated 1st July, eighteen months before she went missing. There were just a few lines explaining what had happened that day. Rebecca had continued adding a few lines each day. Frankly, Sally found it rather mundane and boring. She flicked through several pages. Some entries concerning an August holiday in Devon were a little longer, describing the places they had visited.

As August rolled over to September, she described more about the playgroup she helped at, and her work at The Oaks. She reflected on some of the elderly people she cared for there, and members of their families who visited.

As the days passed, she wrote about preparations for Harvest at the three churches for which David was responsible. As she continued to read Sally learned that there were some discussions in the higher echelons of the diocese about closing Knowle Church and making it into a festival church. Doing so would mean that services would only be held there three or four times a year. Apparently, David was not against the plan as the congregations were so low in numbers - sometimes only six people attended.

Pages turned one by one. Sally felt sleepy. She found nothing to excite her, but continued reading, though she skipped a few entries now and then. Christmas came and went, as did the spring. Easter was clearly a busy time for David, and Rebecca helped as much as she could. Sally glanced at the bedside digital clock radio and noted that it was now twenty-past-twelve: Monday!

The first signs of trouble came in the entries for July. Rebecca wrote about visiting her GP and the doctor's referral to a consultant gynecologist Their summer holiday in Dorset, visiting sites of the Jurassic Coast, was marred by worry. It was not until the entries in September that the tone of the entries took on a sadness. Sally had already learnt that the Staintons could not have children of their own. She became quite emotional as she read Rebecca's words off the page.

As the Harvest Festival season passed again, November came in with a description of a village Bonfire Night celebration on November 5th. Something had changed. The entries were generally about the same length.

However, after some of the entries Rebecca had left a few lines blank. Sally wondered whether Rebecca had intended to return and add more at a later time.

Christmas came with many of the entries similar to the previous year. Carol services were held at the playgroup, The Oaks, the school and, of course, at all three churches.

Another glance at the clock told her it was now nearly half-past one. Greg was sound asleep and snoring!

The entry for Boxing Day told Rebecca's side to the day's events at Knowle. It was glaringly obvious that she was still angry when she wrote that evening. Her part in the protest at the Boxing Day Hunt had begun passively. The actions of the riders and supporters had riled her. She mentioned the incident when a horse had been turned in an aggressive manner with the intention of causing her harm. Fortunately, the act had only been partially successful. Although David had supported her, he was not present as he didn't think it appropriate to be personally involved in the protest. She was back at work the next day.

They celebrated New Year at home in front of the TV with a rare glass of Champagne.

There were more mundane entries until the last one on Tuesday 14th January. Sally flipped through the remaining pages to check that there was nothing else written in the book, then closed it and laid it on the bedside table. She rearranged her pillows, turned the light off and snuggled down to sleep. It was nearly two o'clock. Again!

Sleep eluded her. She was tired, yet her mind was

still active. *There must be something here that I'm missing.* She recalled some of the things she'd read. Eventually sleep came.

Monday 28th May

22

Greg was the first to wake. 'Morning Sal. Sleep well?'

'Err!'

'Come on, wake up,' Greg urged.

'Do I have to?'

'Afraid so. Breakfast in fifteen minutes. I've already showered and shaved.'

Sally dragged herself up to a sitting position. 'I need my coffee.'

'Plenty downstairs.'

'Alright, if I must.'

As she clambered out of bed and made for the bathroom Greg asked, 'How did the reading go?'

'I finished it.'

'Did you learn anything?'

'Not really. I'll tell you later.'

- o0o -

They were a few minutes late for breakfast. Thankfully, Mrs Rawlinson didn't seem to mind. They collected their breakfast from the side table and sat down to eat it.

'So, what did you learn?'

'As I said before, not much. Actually, it was quite boring. It took me until about two o'clock to get to the last entry. I'm not surprised the detectives and Patricia didn't find anything.'

'So you drew a blank.'

'Sorry. Yes. It seems like this has been a wasted journey.'

'Don't say that. Nothing is sometimes something.'

'I guess,' she said with resignation. She took a mouthful of coffee and suddenly spluttered it out across the table just as Vanessa entered the dining room.

The table in front of her was a mess. For that matter, so was Sally. She had coffee down the front of her top and her trousers had caught some as well. She stood up in embarrassment and shock. 'I'm so sorry,' she blurted, and rushed out of the room, closely followed by Greg.

Back in their room, she stripped the coffee-splashed clothes off and rummaged in her bag for the clothes she had worn on the journey north.

'What on earth was that all about?' asked her bewildered husband.

'I suddenly had a thought as I was taking a drink. It shocked me so much that I lost my mouthful of coffee. I'm so ashamed.'

'Forget that. Tell me what thought was so shocking.'

'The blank lines in the diary.'

'What blank lines?'

Sally finished straightening her clothes. 'Later. Let's go finish our breakfast.'

When they reentered the breakfast room, the tablecloth had been changed and Mrs Rawlinson was standing next to the table. Genuinely concerned, she asked, 'Are you alright, sweetie?'

'I'm fine, really, and I'm so sorry about the mess.'

'No problem. These things happen and at least no one died. But I think you'll need to take some fresh coffee and your choice of food.'

'That's very gracious of you. Thank you.'

Sally and Greg collected their second breakfast and sat down.

Vanessa was sitting at the table by the window once more. She looked over. 'I hope it wasn't my entrance that caused that?' she enquired genially.

'No, not at all. Purely coincidental.'

'Well, I'm glad to see you're sorted now.'

'Thanks.' Sally decided to change the subject. 'We were with David Stainton last evening. He told us you were at school together.'

'Yes, I knew you were there. I hope you enjoyed the supper I prepared.'

'We did,' Sally replied, taking in the new information. It certainly made sense of a few things.

'Yes, David left school before I did. Eventually we lost touch. I found him on *Friends Reunited*.'

'And you meet up quite often now?'

'We do. It's been a special time and a privilege to support him over the last few years.'

Greg, who was intrigued and suspicious at the same

time, asked, 'Are you an item?' Sally shot him a reproachful look.

Vanessa laughed. 'An item? I suppose you could call it that. It's complicated.'

'You don't have to explain to us,' Sally said defensively.

'True, but it's no big deal. David is a very honorable person. We are the best of friends... with potential. While there is a chance that Rebecca is alive, he will not allow *us* to be anything other than friends. Should her body be found, then that's another story. Otherwise, we can wait another two-and-a-half years. After seven years, it's assumed that she must have died in one way or another. Either way, I'll be here for him, or out of his life.'

'That must be hard on you.'

'There is *always* hope.' She smiled. 'I have to leave today. My son's with his grandparents. I need to be home to make sure he gets off to his first day at his sixth form collage in the morning - teenagers! And I have to get back to work, more's the pity.'

'Same with us. Before we leave, we need to see David once more.'

Vanessa, who had finished her breakfast stood up and came over to them. She leaned over. 'I'm sure David wouldn't mind. How about having some lunch with us at The Rectory? It won't be anything very spectacular. The shops aren't open today.'

'Well, I don't know.' Sally looked at Greg who responded with a gesture. She understood that it meant:

Why not? 'Well okay then, if you're sure.'

'I'm sure.' She turned to leave. 'See you later.'

-o0o-

They went to their room to finish packing their bags. Greg was anxious for Sally to explain about her 'thought'. 'Come on Sally, tell me now,' he pleaded.

'Right. When I was reading Rebecca's diary, I noticed that she left some blank lines after some of the entries. Over breakfast you said "Nothing is sometimes something." Remember?'

'Yes, I remember.'

'It suddenly struck me. What if the blank lines are not blank?'

'You've lost me.'

'What if she wanted to write something that was so personal that she didn't want anyone at all to read it?'

'Why write something that no one could read?'

'Perhaps she wanted to write it so that if, at some point, she wanted others to read it, she could make it visible.'

'Still makes no sense. How could she do it?'

'Lemon juice.'

'Really?'

'Really!'

'How?'

'Heat it. When I was a Brownie...'

'You never told me you were a Brownie.'

'You never asked. When I was a Brownie, we tried it out. What we did was this. We wrote on a piece of paper with lemon juice. When it was dry it was invisible. To read it we lit a match and warmed it.'

'That sounds dangerous.'

'That's why Brown Owl did that bit for us, and 'Hey Presto' the writing became readable.'

'And you want to light a match on Rebecca's diary. You might burn the book.'

'No. I read somewhere that it's the heat which makes it work and you can heat the paper with an iron.'

'So, you want to iron the diary.'

'Only a few pages.'

'I'm not sure David would like you to iron it.'

'I'll have to ask him first, of course.'

'Better get going then.'

'I'm ready. Let's go.'

- o0o -

Greg settled his bill with Mrs Rawlinson with a generous tip to cover the cost of the breakfast debacle. They drove to The Rectory and were let in by David who was wearing casual attire unlike the black clerical garb of the day before. He welcomed them in and led them to the same room. Vanessa was already there. They had seen her car parked outside. They sat down. Sally was cradling the diary in her arms.

After some small talk, David asked, 'Did you discover anything important in the diary?'

'No, not yet anyway,' Sally replied enigmatically.

'You want to keep it for longer? I really don't want it to leave here.'

'No. You misunderstand. I have a feeling, just a feeling, that there may be some invisible writing.'

'If it's invisible...'

'We make it visible.'

David waved his arm as if holding a magic wand. 'Abracadabra.'

'Not quite.' Sally opened the diary and found an entry that was followed by blank lines. She continued. 'Entries like this one only began in the November.' She passed the diary to Greg, who passed it to David. 'Suppose I'm right and Rebecca wrote with lemon juice...'

'Lemon juice?' David repeated.

'Yes. She'd need a different pen of course.'

'Hang on.' David handed the diary back to Greg, then reached down to his side and lifted the wooden box onto his lap. Opening it up he lifted from it two fountain pens. 'I've tried writing with these. I was puzzled. I wondered why Rebecca had one filled with water. If you're right, it's actually filled with lemon juice, or used to be.'

'How very clever.' Vanessa said. 'I'm impressed. I'm impressed with Rebecca for doing it, and you for solving it.'

Sally was cautious. 'Not quite there yet. We need to warm it up to reveal the writing. What we require, David, is to iron these blank sections and see if anything appears. May we?'

David looked around the room and saw three eager faces staring back at him. 'Well, okay. There's an iron and an ironing board in the old scullery.' He stood up. 'Follow me.' They all trooped out after him.

The scullery had been abandoned as such many years previously. The sinks had been removed and been replaced by a washing machine and a tumble dryer. The iron was sitting on the ironing board. David switched it on at the wall socket. 'Where do we start?'

'Try here,' suggested Sally as she placed the diary on the board. 'This is the first blank section.'

'May I have the honour?' asked Vanessa.

Greg chuckled. 'Rather you than me.'

David stepped back and Vanessa took the iron as the others gathered around. She tapped the plate to check it was hot before carefully gliding the iron over the open page. Lifting the iron they all looked at the page. There was something there, but it was indistinct. She repeated the action more slowly. There was a corporate gasp. The invisible had become visible.

'You *were* right.' David took another step backwards. 'I'll leave you to it because I promised myself I wouldn't read her diary, unless *she* gave me permission. I'll leave you to it.' He left the room.

Vanessa handed the book to Sally who read the once-hidden entry out loud.

'There's something going on. I'm not sure what, but I know it's wrong. I suppose I should mind my own business. Or should I? This could be something big or I could just be imagining things. I wish I knew what to do. How awful!'

The three of them were dumbstruck.

23

While Vanessa held the iron, Sally flicked through the pages of the diary to find the next hidden entry. Once again Vanessa slid the iron over the page causing the writing to appear as if by magic. The second one read:

Today I decided to pay more attention to what he was doing. I can tell he's being very careful. Is it because he doesn't want to be found out? Perhaps I'm being hyper suspicious? Patient observation will determine which.

A week later, Rebecca used her invisible ink to write:

It's happened again. It can't be a coincidence. I think he may have noticed that I've been watching what he's been doing. He's all smiles. Who knows what's going on in his mind.

The week before Christmas she wrote:

Can Christmas ever be the same again? Is it possible that others have seen the same things I've seen? No one is saying anything. What should I do now? Confront him? The consequences could be horrendous.

Then on 26th of December, Boxing Day:

He was at Knowle for the Hunt today. Looking smug. When I was hurt, he could have come to my aid, but he didn't. His true character is well hidden and one day soon, it will be revealed.

The last secret entry was on January 8th:

I've made up my mind. If it happens just once more I'm going to make sure it never happens again. I couldn't live with myself if I did nothing. Watch out Mister. I'm coming for you.

That was the last of the secret entries. The three of them had to decide what to do next. They didn't know who the man was, though Vanessa was absolutely sure that it couldn't be David. Greg and Sally were less sure. They decided to take photos of each of the revealed entries in the hope that it would somehow, sometime, make sense.

'Wait,' said Sally suddenly. 'Can we try one more thing before you turn the iron off? I've just remembered that there are some blank pages at the front. It puzzled me when I saw them last night. I'm wondering if there is something hidden there.'

Vanessa held the iron up ready. 'Sure.' The hot iron revealed nothing on the first page. The second page was full. It was a poem. Sally read it silently. Vanessa put the iron down and unplugged it.

Sally passed the diary on to Greg, who read it and passed it on to Vanessa. When she had finished, she handed it back to Sally.

Vanessa looked to be in a state of turmoil. Eventually she made up her mind. 'This is definitely something that David should see.'

'I agree,' said Sally decisively. 'I'm sure Rebecca intended him to read it. After all, it is addressed to him.' Greg nodded in agreement and the three of them went in search of him. They found him in his study. 'We found this,' said Sally. 'You need to read it.'

'I'm not sure...'

'You need to read it,' she said forcefully as she handed him the diary. He took it and they watched him as he read.

To David

It's said that there's someone for everyone
I wasn't sure 'til I met you;
It's sung that one day my prince will come
In you my dream has come true.

My heart swells at your gentle touch,
It aches when you're not near;
You must know I love you so much
And with me you've nothing to fear.

Only time will tell how our lives will be
I know together we'll get through;
For richer, for poorer united with me
Having all that we need, will do.

Sharing our time while our health prevails
Doing things which enrich our life;
Should sickness strike with all it entails
We'll fight our way through man and wife.

Since being with you I've fallen head over heels
And I love you with all of my heart;
I know you love me and your manner reveals
You and me - till death us do part.

Rebecca ❤

David sank into his chair clutching the diary. He welled up and was stunned into silence. The others, respecting his state of mind, waited for him to compose himself. After several minutes he looked up and began uncertainly. 'It started so well. We were a match made in heaven. I've never hurried into relationships. The first time I met her, I knew that Rebecca was the person I wanted to spend the rest of my life with, Sorry Vanessa.'

'No need to apologise. You were lucky to find her.'

'Then I lost her.'

The silence returned. After a few minutes more, Vanessa excused herself so that she could prepare the promised lunch.

'Did you find anything to help you with your quest?' asked David.

'We found some more hidden entries in the diary. Unfortunately, it has left us with more questions than answers. I've taken some photos of those entries. I hope you don't mind.'

David waved his consent, then changed the subject. 'Do give my best wishes to the people in Whittlebrugh won't you?'

'We will.'

'One more thing,' his tone and expression became serious. 'If you *do* solve the mystery, I want to be the first person you tell. Understand?'

Greg replied for them both. 'Got it.'

'Good.'

-o0o-

Lunch and goodbyes said, Greg and Sally set off for home. The rain pelted down, making the journey really unpleasant. Greg drove while Sally car-dozed.

They arrived at Mark and Rosie's home and spent time with Keily admiring some pictures she had been painting. They stayed for tea before making their way home to Whittlebrugh with Debbie.

Sally persuaded Greg to call Sharon to tell her what they had found out. They still didn't know what had happened to Rebecca, but they were convinced that they needed to find out the identity of the man who was the subject of Rebecca's hidden entries. Was it the same man that Brandon and Ryan had seen getting into the *big* car?

Sharon shared that she had received a call from London. It was the wife, now widow, of Sir Andrew James Greyson 4th Bt., who informed Sharon that her husband, had died having suffered a sudden cardiac arrest. He was eighty-nine years old. It had been his wish to be buried in the family crypt under the North Porch of St Saviour's Church in Knowle. Sharon was to conduct a short service at the crypt burial - a new experience for her.

Tuesday 29th May

24

Bob White left his home in Prospect Terraces to walk to St Saviour's Church. He had been baptised, confirmed, married, and expected to be buried there. As he made his way, something he must have done hundreds, if not thousands of times, he whistled the tune of his favourite hymn: *We love the place, O God, wherein thine honour dwells.*

He had served as churchwarden for twenty-two years. The churchwarden who had shared the responsibility with him for the last two years, was a relative newcomer to Knowle. Joyce lived in one of the new houses that made up the Glebelands Estate. It had only been completed four years earlier. She was the first woman to hold the role at St Saviour's and, although he had had his doubts, she had fulfilled her responsibilities admirably. The Archdeacon, on his recent inspection, had praised them for their work in maintaining the fabric and furnishings *'in such a marvellous manner'.*

His duty on this particular day had come about when the vicar had spoken to him on the phone on Monday evening. He and Joan had just returned from their weekend away at Chetmouth in their caravan. Apparently, Sir Andrew had died suddenly and he was to be laid to rest in the Greyson family crypt. Very few people had ever been in the crypt. It was a little eerie down there amongst the dead. Bob knew it wasn't as bad as people thought, as the coffins were bricked into the coffin-sized chambers after they had been slid into place, feet end first.

He made his way through the graveyard. It was colourful at the time of the year with bluebells under the beech trees on the perimeter. The beech trees and the yew tree by the west door, were showing a blush of young green growth.

He had chosen this particular time because he knew that Derek, the church treasurer, would be there to collect the cash from the safe to deposit it at the bank. Derek had already unlocked the vestry door and switched the lights on. Bob entered. There was a chill in the building. It caused him to shiver.

'Good morning, Derek,' he said cheerily.

'Morning Bob. I'm just about to leave. Alright?'

'No problem, but before you lock the safe, I need the crypt key. I have to check the crypt for Sharon. There's a new resident expected soon with the death of Sir Andrew.'

'Oh. Right. Well, carry on.'

The safe was set into the wall. The right-hand drawer at the bottom held a tin with a collection of various keys. Bob reached behind the tin - the place where the over-sized Greyson Crypt key was kept. He felt around.

'It's not there,' he exclaimed in a startled tone. He

took out the tin and checked the void visually. He checked inside the tin and returned it to its place before opening the left-hand drawer. Still nothing!

Derek saw his anxiety and decided to join in with the search. The search continued as, now rather concerned, they removed the registers, books and silverware from the main part of the safe. No key. They replaced all the items and stood back in complete confusion. *Where on earth had it gone?*

Derek relocked the safe as Bob frantically started to search the desk drawers. Anxiety rose as the search and the time progressed.

Eventually he pulled out his mobile and rang Joyce. 'Hi Joyce, it's Bob. I'm at church. I need to find the key for the crypt. Have you any idea where it is?'

'If it's not in the safe drawer, then I have no idea. It's the big one with the Greyson motif on it, isn't it?'

'Yes, that's the one.'

'Have you checked both drawers?'

'Yes.'

'In that case, I can't help you.'

'Okay. I'll check with Sharon. Thanks anyway. Bye.'

Bob rang Sharon's mobile. It rang a few times before going to voicemail. 'Hi Sharon. Bob here. Ring me back when you can. I think we have a problem. Bye.'

He and Derek had a quick look around the rest of the building to make sure everything was in order. Then exited the building, checking everything was locked on the way out. As they passed the North Porch, Bob checked the crypt door situated on the east side. He tried the handle and shook the door. It didn't budge. He glanced above the door at the carving of the Greyson motif of a letter 'G' entwined with a Staffordshire Knot.

As they parted Bob thanked Derek for his help. 'I hope we don't have to break into the crypt. I just can't imagine who would have removed the key, and why.'

'Good luck, Bob.'

'Thanks.'

They parted and Bob retraced his steps to Prospect Terraces. He had just opened his front door when his mobile rang. He checked to see who it was, and seeing it was Sharon, answered quickly.

'Morning Bob. Sorry I missed your call. What can I do for you?'

'Vicar, I can't find the key to the crypt!'

'You've checked the safe?'

'I've checked *everywhere*. Derek was there to collect the cash for the bank. He helped me search.' His anxiety was evident in his voice.

'Are there any copies?'

'Not to my knowledge.'

'So we need to find it.'

'Or break in.'

'Let's hope it doesn't come to that. Who has access to the safe?'

'Not many people – the wardens, the treasurer, the sacristan and you.'

'When was the crypt last opened?'

'The last time is likely to have been when Sir Timothy's widow was laid to rest in the late 70s. I think I was in my early twenties. I seem to remember it was about the time of our Queen's Silver Jubilee celebrations. That was umm... June 1977.'

'Have you seen the key since then?'

'I'm pretty sure it was there recently, but I can't be sure.'

'Okay. I'll have a think. Could you ask around. I'm sure it'll turn up. Mind you we've only got a few days.'

'I'll do my best.'

'Take care now. We'll talk again soon.'

'Thanks. Goodbye.'

Joan had been listening in to one end of the conversation. 'Sounds like a big problem, Bob.'

'Yes. It's not good.'

'Sit down, my dear. I'll make you a cup of tea. Maybe you'll find a solution by the time you've had a rest.'

'Thank you, sweetheart. I do hope so.'

- o 0 o -

Sharon popped her mobile back into her pocket as she considered the problem. She had never seen the crypt key. There had been no need for her to visit the Greyson Crypt. She had no idea what it was like. Now she had a good reason to see it for herself and she couldn't - not yet anyway. She went about her duties for the day. It was a short week due to the Bank Holiday so she had to squeeze a lot of work into fewer days. Nevertheless, she was at home when Simon arrived from work. She explained the problem of the missing key to Simon.

'You could always bring in a locksmith or... do you know any professional burglars?'

'Very funny. Not helpful.'

'Sorry.'

They finished their evening meal and sat down to watch an episode of an American police detective series.

'Wait a minute. I've just had an idea,' said Simon.

'Do you want to watch something else?'

'No, I want to go for a walk.'

'Really?'

'Really. You may be delighted with the result.'

'Where are we going?'

'You'll see. Come on.'

25

Simon led Sharon across Church Road to the entrance of The Red Lion. 'A drink in here?' said Sharon who was clearly disappointed. 'We could have poured a drink at home and enjoyed it in front of the TV.'

'We aren't going in for a drink.'

'Then what?'

'You'll see.' He pushed the door open and led her to the bar. 'Hi Terry. Do you mind if we take a closer look at your keys, the ones up there?' He pointed to the ceiling beams.

'Knock yourselves out.'

'Thanks.'

Sharon looked up to see the collection of old keys hanging on nails along the length of the old black-painted beams. There were small and large keys; some simple and some intricate; some old and some modern.

'Now, Sharon, let's see if the crypt key is here.'

'Why would it be?'

'We'll ask that if we find it. What does it look like?'

'I'm not sure. Give me a minute. I'll call Bob.' Sharon stepped outside and made the call. She was back in under two minutes with a smile on her face. 'Easy. Bob tells me it's unique. It's about eight inches long and has the Greyson motif on the handle - a letter 'G' with the Staffordshire Knot.'

'Okay. You start at that end, and I'll start at this end. We'll meet in the middle.'

'I won't be able to reach that high.'

'Just look for now. If you see it, we'll ask Terry to lend us a step ladder or something. Go girl.'

They made their way to opposite ends of the room. There were something like thirty keys on each side of each beam. As they knew what to look for, it was simple to scan the beams. Sharon had the end with the central fireplace, so had to double back to check the other side. It still took less than a minute to complete the search. 'Got it,' she called victoriously.

Several customers looked up to see her pointing to a key hanging at the bar end of the beam. Simon reached up on tiptoes He still wasn't tall enough to reach it, so he grabbed a nearby chair and climbed on it. He lifted the key off the nail, climbed down and handed it to Sharon.

'Your key, I think, Madam.'

Sharon examined it. The motif was just as Bob described - a 'G' with a Staffordshire Knot. 'Looks like it.'

Terry leaned over the bar. 'What have you got there, Vicar?'

'I believe this is the key to the Greyson Crypt at Knowle church.'

'Well, I'll be blowed! That's the latest addition to my collection. It's only been up there for a week or so.'

Sharon was intrigued. 'Where did it come from?'

'Cliff and Tony brought it in. They found it with the magnet thing in the canal.'

'Is that Cliff Johnson who discovered the bomb?'

'The very same.'

'That's one mystery solved and another one begun. How did a key that was locked in the Knowle church safe end up in the canal?'

'Well,' said Terry with a wry smile, 'some might call it magic, whereas you might call it a miracle.'

'No Terry. It would be a miracle if it floated.'

'If you say so. I suppose you want to keep it.'

'Of course. We need it.' Sharon explained. 'You may not have heard yet. Sir Andrew Greyson's died. He's to join other members of his family in the Crypt. This key will get us in.'

'Can I have the key back afterwards?'

'Sorry, no. It will be returned to the church and kept securely until the next Greyson has need of it.'

Simon butted in. 'I think we ought to get off home Sharon. You need to call Bob and put him out of his misery.' Sharon agreed. She called Bob as they walked back to The Vicarage and gave him the good news. He was delighted. She told him that they needed to find out who took the key from the safe and threw it into the canal. He agreed. 'I'll get back to you on that,' she promised.

Wednesday 30th May

26

Early on Wednesday morning, Sharon drove over to Knowle Church to test the key out on the crypt door. The lock was stiff from disuse. She managed to turn the key causing a rasping sound. *Definitely needs some oil.*

She pulled the door open and found an old wooden platform leading to a wooden staircase descending to the right. She took out her mobile and turned on the light to act as a torch, then proceeded gingerly into the void. Cobwebs tickled her face and hair. The stairs creaked.

When she reached the bottom, she found herself in a room. Along the wall to her left she could see three rows, one row above the other, each of seven chambers. The coffin-sized chambers extended further into the void. Counting from the top, there were eleven bricked-up chambers, leaving ten yet to be used for family members. It fascinated her to see that water dripping from the ceiling had formed several thin, white stalactites.

She checked the time and was relieved to find that she should leave to prepare for the mid-week service in the church itself. If she didn't have a reason to leave, she would have made one up just to leave quickly. She ascended the stairs and exited, locking the door behind her.

Bob, who had watched her lock the door, greeted her. 'Morning Vicar. Everything alright down there?'

'Looks fine to me. I've been thinking. Let's call a meeting for this evening, of all the people who have access to the safe, and see if we can figure out who removed the key, and why.'

-o0o-

On Wednesday afternoon, having returned home for his usual half-day off, Greg completed his domestic chores, before preparing to go for a walk. Debbie became excited as soon as he took her lead off the hook by the kitchen door. He checked the weather through the window. It looked fair, so he slung his waterproof coat over his shoulder in case it should begin to rain again.

He was soon making his way towards the centre of the village with Debbie, as usual, pulling ahead. The village was quiet as if everyone was taking a Spanish-style siesta. He turned into Smithy Lane.

As he approached the almshouses, he saw a nurse about to leave Jack Taylor's home. Jack, who was standing at his open door, noticed Greg and gave him a wave. Greg waved back, but was surprised when Jack beckoned him to come over.

'Greg, do you know Gladys Wilcox, our District Nurse?'

'I don't think we've met,' said Greg somewhat puzzled.

'Then that's a good thing. She only visits the sick and dying.'

'I only visit the nicest people,' she responded with a smile and a broad accent. Greg suspected it originated in the West Indies. The accent matched her appearance. 'You live nearby, eh, Mister... ?'

'Williams. Greg Williams. We live just up the road. This is Debbie,' he said as he tried to keep his dog from jumping up.

'Nice to meet you, Greg, and you Debbie.'

'Greg and his wife are trying to find out what happened to Rebecca Stainton.' Jack explained. 'They're the reason for all the pink bows you see in the village.'

'Oh, now I see.' She spoke tenderly to Greg. 'I knew Rebecca a little. She worked up at The Oaks. She was a nice young lady. It was so sad to hear she was missing. I think she knew one of our GPs, Doctor Edwards who attended there quite often.'

'I think I heard of him when we visited The Oaks.'

'You may well have done.'

'I'd rather be at home being looked after by Gladys than in *that* place,' Jack said scornfully. 'It's just a waiting room for heaven, or hell.'

'You're right Mr Taylor,' said Gladys. 'Much better where you are. I much prefer that you are here where I can keep my eye on you. Though now, I must leave you. I have more visits to make. Goodbye Greg. Goodbye Debbie. Nice to meet you both.' She turned and headed to her car.

'Are you going to come in?' asked Jack.

'I better not. Debbie will leave hair everywhere. But thank you. So, how are you doing?'

'I'm not the young man I once was, that's for sure. And I've got some nasty sores - you really don't want to know where! That's why Gladys comes to see me. She's quite a dear.'

'I can tell.'

'Have you found out any more about Rebecca?'

'A little, though nothing conclusive. We know she was concerned about the actions of a man. Trouble is, we don't know what actions they were nor who he was. There's one thing we do know. This mystery man was at Knowle's Boxing Day Hunt a few weeks before she disappeared.'

'That should narrow it down.'

Greg pulled his mobile out and found the pictures he had taken of Bob's photos from the Hunt. 'Have a look at these. You may recognise some of the people.'

Jack leaned his walking stick against the door frame and looked through the pictures as Greg scrolled through them. 'Who took them?'

'Bob White.'

'That figures. I noticed Joan White in the crowd. There's a few of Rebecca. Joyce Shilton is there. She's the other churchwarden at St Saviour's. Terry Williams. He's something up at Blakeley's Golf Club. Caroline Carter. She and Richard run the fruit and veg shop in the old hall gardens. This is Doctor Edwards who we've just been talking about. He lives just around the corner from The Green.' He looked up as he remembered something. 'Do you remember when they used to have a Maypole Dance on The

Green on Mayday each year? Haven't done that for a while.'

'Any others?'

Jack looked at another photo. 'That's Derek Ballard, the Church Treasurer. And I think that's Carl Tucker. His dad was the village baker back in the day.'

He pointed to a rider in another photo. 'Wow! If I'm not very much mistaken, that's John Greyson, Sir Andrew's grandson. He looks just like his grandfather. Actually, that's not right. Have you heard? Sir Andrew has died. John's father is now Sir Christopher because he now holds the title.'

'Yes. Sharon said something about that.'

Jack finished going through the photos. 'That's about all. I don't know the newcomers so much.'

'That's been very helpful. Thank you.'

'No problem.' Jack handed the mobile back and retrieved his walking stick.

'Well, I hope your sores clear up soon.'

'Me too, though if they do, I won't get to see the nurse so often.'

'Always a down side isn't there?'

Jack chuckled. 'Soon I expect to be in a far better place.'

'Are you moving? The Oaks?'

'God forbid. I meant my *heavenly* home.'

'Oh. Not too soon I hope.'

'I've had a good innings. I hope you find out what happened to Rebecca. I'd like to know that.'

'Me too. Take care now.'

Jack gave a feeble wave and turned to re-enter his home. Greg and Debbie continued their walk around the block counting the pink bows as they went.

27

By the time Sally arrived home from work, Greg had written a list of all the names he could remember of the people who had been at the Boxing Day Hunt.

'Do you think it's one of them?' asked Sally.

'There's a good chance. Though if one of the men in the list is the person Rebecca was concerned about, it doesn't follow that he was the man in the *big* car, or the person responsible for her disappearance.'

'So, should we concentrate on these?'

'Yes. I'm wondering if any of them have a big car.'

'Well, we could investigate one of them tonight.'

'Who do you suggest?'

'We haven't investigated Rex.'

'Ah, yes, Rex Marshall, the aggressive horseman.'

'Exactly. So, after we've had something to eat, how about we pop over to Knowle and see if we can find him. Forest View, wasn't it?'

'I think so. Okay, if we must.'

'It's important to follow up every avenue just in case we miss something. Bob seemed to be quite sure he might be capable of something violent.'

'Then we better tread carefully.'

-o0o-

The drive was brief. They turned into Forest View and stopped by the kerb. 'So where is the forest?' asked Greg.

'No idea. Unless it refers to the wood beyond the field behind the houses.'

'Where to now?'

'Door to door?'

'Okay. I'll take the right-hand side, you the left.'

'Fine, but make sure we stay in sight of each other.'

Off they went to knock on doors.

Sally had reached Number 6 before she found out anything useful. She crossed the road to where Greg was just about to go to his third door. 'Got it Greg,' she called. 'Number eleven is where Rex and his mother live.'

They walked up the road and to the door of Number 11. Sally rang the bell. She was a little nervous, so she pushed Greg forward. A lady on the upper side of sixty answered the door.

'Yes?'

'Hi. My name is Greg Williams and this is my wife, Sally. Is Rex in?'

'No. Why?'

'We were wondering if we might have a word with him.'

'He's away at the moment. I'm his mother.'

'When will he be back?'

'Friday night. What's this about?'

'We're looking into the mystery of Rebecca Stainton's disappearance. We know he met her at the Boxing Day Hunt. We thought he might have some information that didn't come to light before.'

'Are you anything to do with all those pink bows going up everywhere?'

'That's us,' said Sally, with more confidence than she felt.

'It's a long time ago. I'm not sure he'll even remember anything.'

'Do you remember if he joined in the search for Rebecca?'

'Let me think...

'It was January fifteenth.'

'Wait, yes I do remember something now.'

'Yes?' Sally said hopefully.

'Actually, Rex was off work that week. He had man flu. Was in bed for several days, making something out of nothing if you ask me. Anyway, when he heard there was someone missing, he called a few of his friends, pulled himself out of bed, and they went into the wood, searched it for hours.'

'That was on the day she went missing?'

'No, the day after. He hadn't left his bed for two or three days before that. He took the rest of that week off. Back to work the week after.'

'Where does he work?'

'Here and there. He drives heavy plant, you know those giant yellow vehicles they use in road construction and the like. He stays away most weeks in his van.'

'A van?'

'Yes. He's got one of those VW things. A camper van. He sleeps in it when he's away. Saves all the cost of paying for accommodation.'

'Oh.' Sally and Greg looked at each other.

'Well thank you. You've been most helpful. Sorry to have troubled you.'

'Yes, thank you,' added Sally. 'Have a good evening.'

As they made their way back to their car Greg said, 'Well, I think that removes him from the list of potential suspects.'

'Never mind. At least we tried.'

28

Sharon sat at the end of the table in the vestry of St Saviour's Church. Also sitting at the table were Bob and Joyce, the churchwardens; Derek Ballard, the church treasurer; Brenda Coates, the sacristan; and Grace Brown, the Church Council secretary.

'Thank you all for coming this evening at such short notice. I wanted to get you all together to try and solve the mystery of the crypt key. As most of you will have heard, the key was recently dragged up from the mud at the bottom of the canal near the bridge on Knowle Lane. I found it among the keys hanging on the beams in The Red Lion. What I want to know is, how did it get there?'

All those sitting around the table looked at each other curiously.

Sharon continued. 'I understand from Bob, that the key was kept here in the safe drawer. It must have been used for the last burial. That would have been for....' She looked to Bob for help.

'Patience Greyson, Sir Timothy's widow, in 1977.'

'Thank you. When did it disappear and who took it? You all have access to the safe. Anyone own up?'

Silence. Sharon looked around the table. All eyes

were on her. Either they were all innocent or someone was hiding their guilt effectively. 'Okay. Let's try another tack. If it wasn't one of you, who else has had the opportunity to remove the key from the safe?'

Bob cleared his throat. 'Since 1977 we have had three vicars before you: Ian Cooper, Benedict Downley and David Stainton. All of them had access to the safe. We've also had a number of treasurers, churchwardens, and a couple of sacristans.'

'Point taken.'

'There is also the possibility,' began Derek, 'that it was someone who came into the vestry while the safe was unlocked.'

'When is the safe left unlocked?' asked a scandalised Sharon.

'Before, during and after every service.'

'Really? How come?'

'I'm normally the person who opens the safe,' admitted Brenda. 'I need to prepare the items for Holy Communion. I leave it open because I know others will want to access it. After the service I put the silver back. The collection is often being counted at the same time, so I don't lock it. I leave that to the treasurer.'

Bob continued the explanation. 'It's custom for the last person in church to check that the main door is secured, the safe is locked, and all the lights are turned off. You do that sometimes, don't you Vicar?'

Sharon blushed. 'I do. So, what you're suggesting is that, during the last forty or so years, any member of the congregation could have had access to the safe and removed the key.'

'Exactly.'

'Oh dear. We're no nearer finding the culprit now than when we started.'

'I think I can narrow it down,' said Brenda timidly. All eyes turned to her. 'I'm pretty sure the crypt key was in the safe drawer during David's time. I seem to remember that he couldn't find the baptism spoon, you know, the fancy silver spoon about the same size as a teaspoon, but with a long handle. He and I searched the safe together. We eventually found it in its felt bag behind one of the drawers. That's when I saw the key for the first, no, for the *only* time.'

'Only seven or eight years to consider then,' reflected Sharon despondently.

'Does it really matter now that we have the key back in the safe?' asked Bob.

'I guess not, though it remains a mystery. However, I think we ought to review procedures to make sure that nothing can be taken from the safe without another person's knowledge.'

Heads nodded in agreement, though no one was able to suggest how things could be done differently.

-o0o-

When the meeting had been concluded and everyone had left, Sharon checked the main door, checked the safe, turned all the lights off, and locked the vestry door.

She unlocked her car and sat in it. The thing that was now exercising her mind was that, as well as not knowing *who* had taken the key from the safe, she still had no idea *why* someone would have taken the key; and more than that, why they would have disposed of it by throwing it into the canal.

She started the engine and moved away from the kerb. As the month of May was drawing to a close and June was just around the corner, the evening was bright and pleasant. The yellow of so many dandelions in the verges had been replaced by an abundance of buttercups intermingling with the mystical spheres of dandelion seed heads.

She drove out of the village and across the canal bridge before coming to the 'T' junction with Church Road. She waited for a supermarket delivery van to pass, then continued to The Vicarage.

As she pulled into her driveway, she wondered how Greg and Sally were doing with the other mystery. It had been nearly a month since she asked them to find out about Rebecca. The only thing to show for it was the display of pink ribbon bows and the possible lead about a man in a 'big' car. *Was that all that would be discovered? Surely not.*

Thursday 31st May

29

Nurse Gladys, having completed her morning list, called in at The Oaks Nursing Home on the off-chance of having a word with the manager.

Her demeanor signaled to Gordon that a confidential conversation was envisaged, so he invited her into his office.

'This is rather delicate,' Gladys began. 'I trust that I can speak openly in confidence.'

'Of course. What's this about?'

'I have a concern. I can't prove anything - it's no more than a suspicion.' She closed her eyes and drew a deep breath. Gordon waited. 'Do you think there is any possibility that some of your patients may be passing before their rightful time?'

Gordon pulled himself up straight. 'Is there an accusation in there, because I can assure you that we do all we can for the wellbeing of our...'

'... No. No. You misunderstand. It's not about you or the staff here.'

'Then what are you saying?'

Gladys drew breath once again. Her face showed that she was in a turmoil. 'Look, I attend chronic and critical ill patients in the community. Doctor Edwards also attends when necessary. It may be just coincidental, but...' she sighed and looked directly into Gordon's eyes. '...some of my patients passed, I believe prematurely, soon after they'd received a visit from the doctor.'

Gordon leaned back into his chair and stroked his beard. He pondered for a while before responding. 'That is a *very* serious accusation. It implies criminal activity.'

'A suspicion, not an accusation.'

'Semantics.'

'I don't want to cause a fuss especially as I have no proof. I thought you would be a person to lay out my suspicions as, if there is something going on, you may have similar things happening with your patients. Have you?'

'I can assure you that, if we had any suspicions at all, we would take action to make sure that the situation was thoroughly investigated. We take great pride in the duty of care for all who come to The Oaks.'

'Have you?'

'I can categorically state that I am unaware of any patient who has passed *prematurely*, as you put it.'

'That, I have to say, is a great relief.' She relaxed. 'I must be wrong. Thank you for your assurance.'

'I'm glad to set your mind at rest. I did hear that Doctor Edwards has a certain compassion for the dying coming from his personal experience with his elderly father who, if I remember correctly, had cancer and dementia - a horrible thing for all concerned. Sadly, situations like that are not so uncommon nowadays as we know all too well.'

'Indeed.'

'Nevertheless, to set our minds completely at rest, I will speak to Daisy, to see if she has any concerns in this area. It would be totally negligent on our part should we miss something so serious. Pray God we haven't. In the meantime, let's keep this within the walls of this room. No point in 'crying wolf'.'

'Thank you so much for your time.' Gladys rose from her seat.

'No problem.'

Gladys left the building a lot happier than when she arrived. Meanwhile, Gordon called the nurses' room and asked his Nursing Officer, Daisy Chambers, to come to see him when she had a moment.

Gordon spun his chair around and looked out of the window. Nurse Gladys was driving down the drive in her little Nissan Micra. His own Toyota Land Cruiser was parked under his window. In the sunshine he noted that it was due for a wash. He smiled to himself and turned as he heard a knock on his door.

'Come in.'

The door opened and Daisy entered. 'You wanted to see me.'

'Yes. Just a quick one. Have you *any* concerns about the treatment our patients are receiving from Doctor Edwards?'

'Umm. No, I don't think so. I can't think of anything. Why?'

'Just checking.'

'Has someone said something?'

'I can't say.'

'But you won't deny it.'

'Publicly I would. It's obviously a delicate situation.'

'I believe Doctor Edwards is a competent and caring practitioner. It sounds to me as if someone is trying to start a malicious rumour.'

'At least we have no qualms about his visits here. That's the main thing. But,' he hesitated, 'you might keep a watchful eye out when he visits.'

'Of course.'

'Thank you. That's all.'

-o0o-

Daisy mulled over the conversation she'd had with the Manager. She had caught sight of the District Nurse leaving The Oaks minutes before she was summoned to Gordon's office. She decided that the two things must be connected - one a consequence of the other. She hadn't even considered that Jason Edwards' work was in the least questionable. Not, that is, until the suggestion had been made.

During the rest of her shift her mind kept coming back to the doctor. She pondered what concerns might have been raised. It also occurred to her that, if he was implicated in some way, she might also be implicated by association. That was scary. The more she thought about it, the more worried she became.

By the time she came to the end of her shift and the handover to the late shift, she was in quite a state. Even at handover her mood was noticed, especially as she was in a haste to leave. She brushed off concern shown towards her and was relieved to leave for home.

As she drove through the gateway she noticed, not for the first time, the pink ribbons tied to the gates, the cards and the bouquet of, now dead, flowers. However, they made a particular impression on her as she remembered that the last conversation she had had with Gordon, was a week or so back. That was when a couple from the village had been asking about Rebecca Stainton because they wanted to find out what had happened to her.

She stopped at the village shop to buy some milk. In the window she noticed a small poster asking anyone who had information about Rebecca's disappearance to contact Greg and Sally Williams. This, she remembered, was the couple who had visited The Oaks. She took a note of the telephone number. When she returned to the car, milk in hand, she made a split decision to return to The Oaks. She wasn't quite sure if she was doing the right thing, but she knew if she didn't do this straight away, she probably wouldn't do it. Ever.

30

Daisy, having left her car on Church Road, entered through the main door as usual. She had noted that Gordon's car was not in his parking space. She checked that no one was around before heading straight for the staircase to the first floor. She dived into the Records Room at the rear of the building.

After closing the door behind her, she turned on the fluorescent light. Hanging in the centre of the windowless room, it was the only source of illumination. It was a small space with five four-drawer grey cabinets on opposite sides, making her feel claustrophobic.

She looked at the cabinets. Each of the drawers had a label holder with a card in place indicating its contents. The five cabinets on her left were for *Patient Records* arranged in alphabetical order. She became aware of the musty smell exaggerated by the isolation. At that moment it felt more like in a prison cell than anything else.

On a small desk, pressed up against the wall opposite the door, lay an open A4 hardcover notebook. It was used to record details of each patient when their files were archived. Daisy went straight to it, sat in the office chair, and started flicking back through the pages. She knew that the Administrator, Karen, entered the details of each patient's file when it was archived in this room. This was done shortly after a patient left or died.

She found the entries for six years previous. The entries listed the full name; date of birth; date of arrival and date of 'departure'; next of kin; and, if relevant, name of staff member, or members, present at time of death.

Placing her forefinger on the page, she drew it downwards as she scanned the entries. When she had finished one page, she moved to the next until she found what she was looking for. It was dated 16th March and the staff member present at death was recorded as Rebecca Stainton. Taking note of the patient's name, she stood and moved to the cabinet where the patient's file was stored. The cabinet was locked.

Feeling rather foolish, she sat back down at the table with her head in her hands. *Think, think, think.* She realised that the keys must be with Karen, whose office was at the front of the building, at the far end of the landing, on the other side of the staircase. *In for a penny, in for a pound.*

She checked her watch. It was already eight minutes to five. Karen worked office hours: 9 to 5, though she was known to leave early quite often. Daisy decided to wait for a few minutes just in case this was one of the days Karen didn't leave early. The second hand on her watch seemed to move in slow motion as she sat silently at the desk. The nurse in her became aware of her own pulse. It was much faster than was normal.

At five-past five she went to the door, switched the

light off, and cautiously cracked open the door a few inches. She couldn't hear anything so she pulled it open further until she could see that the way was clear. That established, she stealthily made her way to Karen's office.

The window of the Admin Office faced west so the room was filled with light making her task of finding the cabinet keys easier. She sat in Karen's chair and checked the drawers, feeling a bit like a thief, and stopping regularly to listen out for sounds of anyone approaching.

The keys were not to be found at the desk, so she looked around the room. Her eyes fell on a metal box attached to the wall to the side of the light switch. She made her way to it and found it had a lock. It crossed her mind that she would be beaten if the cabinet keys were locked inside. Nevertheless, she tried to open it and, to her amazement, found that it was unlocked. Inside were an assortment of keys neatly labeled, one bunch of small keys were marked as 'Patient Records'. Daisy quickly unhooked them and made her way back, showing the same caution.

She unlocked the five cabinets before checking the first file. Then she returned to the table and continued the search. Every time she spotted Rebecca's name she pulled the patient's file, made a note on a page she had torn from the back of the patient record notebook, and returned the file to the cabinet. The page was filling up, but when she came to the January of Rebecca's disappearance, she closed the book knowing that her name would not be recorded again.

Her retreat was as careful as her entrance. Clasping

the sheet of paper she had been writing on, she made sure that everything looked the same as it had on her arrival. She returned the keys to Karen's office then sneaked to the top of the staircase where she waited in case anyone might be in the hallway below. No one was, so she tiptoed down the stairs and continued out of the building and along the drive to her car.

Daisy sat silently in the car for a while. She was astonished to find that it was twenty-past seven. She pulled out her mobile and called the number she had noted from the poster in the village shop and waited for someone to answer.

-o0o-

The ringtone of Greg's mobile, backed by the vibration, caught him as he was attempting to adjust the door of one of the kitchen cupboards - something Sally had been nagging him to do for several weeks. He took the mobile from his pocket and looked at the screen. He didn't recognise the number. He answered it with an innocuous way expecting it to be a sales call.

He heard a woman's voice. 'Is that Mr Williams?'

'Who's asking?'

'I'm Daisy. I work at The Oaks Nursing Home. We met a few weeks back.'

'Good evening, Daisy. How can I help you?'

'I read the poster about Rebecca. I *think* I can help you.'

'Oh!'

'Is it possible for us to meet up?'

'Of course. When?'

'Now.'

'Wow. Okay. I'm at home. Would you like to come here?'

'I can do that.'

'I'll be waiting. Sixty-two Church Road.'

'Thanks. See you in a mo.' The phone went dead.

Greg returned to the cupboard and closed the door and examined it. It was still crooked.

Sally came in from the lounge. 'Who was that?'

'Daisy from The Oaks. She's coming to see us.'

They had been planning to sit down and watch the fourth semi-final of *Britain's Got Talent.* Greg just had time to explain to her about the phone call when the doorbell rang. Greg opened the door. He recognised Daisy from their visit to The Oaks - helped by the fact that she was wearing her nurse's uniform.

He led her into the lounge and invited her to sit. Sally offered her a drink. She declined. In her hand she was clutching a piece of paper. It was covered with handwriting.

'First of all,' Daisy said nervously, 'I want to thank you for trying to find out what happened to Rebecca. We really liked her. She was a good worker and a very caring person.' Greg and Sally, now seated on the sofa, nodded in acknowledgement. 'I think I may have something, but I could be completely wrong.'

Daisy's voice was trembling, as were her hands. Greg and Sally waited hopefully. Daisy waited for a moment and then, to their surprise, asked a question. 'Have *you* found out anything that might lead you to suspect anyone responsible for Rebecca's disappearance?'

They looked at each other, uncertain how much to tell Daisy. Eventually Greg began. 'We have discovered a couple of things that might point towards someone, but as yet we don't know who that might be.'

'Can you be more specific? It's important.'

Greg looked at Sally who nodded and continued. 'We understand that Rebecca had her suspicions about a man who was doing something she deemed as wrong. We've also learnt that, on the evening of her disappearance, she was seen with a man wearing a hat and coat who drove her, in a big car, towards Knowle.'

'Mary, mother of Jesus,' Daisy whispered as she crossed herself. Greg and Sally were startled at her reaction. They waited. Daisy fiddled with the paper she was holding in her hands. She didn't look up as she spoke again. 'I had a strange conversation this afternoon. It made me do some thinking. That led me to consider a possibility to do with Rebecca. I did some research before I phoned you. It matches what you've just told me. I dearly hope I'm wrong for pity's sake.'

'Let's hear it,' said Greg impatiently.

'I don't know. It's too awful to put it into words.'

'I tell you what,' assured Sally, 'you tell us what you're thinking and we'll do our very best to confirm or disprove your suspicions. And I promise that what you say here will be treated in the utmost confidence. Okay?'

Daisy pulled a tissue from her pocket, removed her glasses, and dabbed at her eyes. She replaced her glasses, looked at the Williamses and murmured, 'Okay.'

-o0o-

Sharon was just settling down after a busy evening completing a baptism preparation interview with a couple who lived in Caulston, when the house phone rang. She had forgotten to turn her phone back on having completed the visit, so she turned it back on as she walked into her study to answer the call. She checked her wall clock and noticed that it had gone nine.

'Sharon, thank God. We've been trying to reach you.'

'Who is this?'

'Greg. We need your help and advice. It's about Rebecca.' Greg sounded breathless with excitement.

'Calm down, Greg. Tell me what's happening.'

'Not on the phone. We need to meet - soon.'

'Do you want to come here now, or can it wait?'

'Now would be good. See you in a few minutes.'

The line went dead leaving Sharon bewildered. She went back to the living room and explained to Simon that she was having some late evening visitors. He tutted. 'I'll be here if you need me. Not too late now. You have a full day tomorrow.'

'I know. Thanks, Love.'

She heard the Williamses' car on the drive as she put the kettle on in the kitchen. She opened the door and ushered Greg and Sally into her study. 'Tea's on its way. Back in a jiff.'

31

Greg's eyes were drawn to the picture on the wall. He had noticed it on his first visit to the study. He remembered that Sharon had told him that it was Salvador Dali's *Christ of Saint John of the Cross*. He looked around and observed the bookshelves covering the whole of one wall.

Sharon came in with three mugs and placed them on a coffee table. 'I see you're impressed with my books. I've actually read some of them.' She grinned. 'I'm told that removal workers especially fear moving clergy and lawyers as they tend to have the most books.'

Sharon spun her office chair around from her desk so that she was facing the sofa. Greg and Sally were perched on the edge of their seats in obvious agitation. 'So, what is so important that it couldn't wait and you couldn't speak about it on the phone?'

Greg cleared his throat before beginning. 'We've just heard from someone who thinks they may have discovered what was troubling Rebecca. I think I told you about the hidden entries in her diary when I phoned you on Monday.'

'You did.'

'Right. Well, she wrote about a man who was doing

something she believed was very wrong. If reported, it would have horrendous consequences. The person who spoke to us wants to remain anonymous, but I can tell you that the person worked with Rebecca at The Oaks.'

Sharon leaned forward anxious to hear what Greg had to say next.

'This person has looked at the records of residents during the time that Rebecca worked there. Our informant discovered that Rebecca was present during the last moments of the lives of a number of the residents. She suspects that Rebecca was concerned that those lives were cut short in a compassionate, but illegal way.'

Sharon gasped. 'Who would do that?'

'Well that's the rub.'

'The thing is,' observed Sally, 'if this person Rebecca was suspicious of, knew that she was about to accuse him of an illegal practice, it might well give a motive for murder, though that would be extreme for someone who was clearly compassionate.'

'So, come on. Who are we talking about? Someone at The Oaks?'

'Kind of,' Greg said hesitantly. 'The other person present with Rebecca on a number of occasions when a resident breathed their last was... the doctor.'

'Doctor Jason Edwards,' blurted Sally.

All three of them collapsed back in their seats as if they had been suddenly stunned by a poisonous gas.

'Wow!' uttered Sharon, in surprise and shock.

'Exactly.'

'Is there any proof?'

'Only circumstantial,' admitted Greg.

'I know Jason a little. He's a member of the congregation at St Saviour's. He always seems so caring. I find it difficult to believe that he could be another Harold Shipman.'

'I don't think Dr Edwards is in the same league,' said Sally aghast. 'If I remember rightly, Shipman murdered over two hundred patients most of whom were elderly women in good health.'

'And our informant,' added Greg, 'says that all of those who died at The Oaks were seriously ill and would have died hours or days later anyway.'

'Still doesn't make it right though, does it?' insisted Sharon. All three remained in silent, reflective thought for several minutes. 'Where do we go from here?'

'That's why we've come to you,' explained Sally. 'You set us on this quest. We need your advice.'

'Do we go to the police?' asked Greg.

Sharon sucked through her teeth like a builder does when he's about to give an expensive quote for some work. 'I don't think we're there yet. Let's see. We have the suspicion of a *motive*. Right?'

'Right,' they chorused.

'Do we have a *means*?'

'No,' Greg said defensively. 'We don't even have a body.'

'Did Jason have the *opportunity* to murder her?'

'Yes,' Sally said defiantly, 'if he was the man in the big

car seen driving off with her.'

'And,' added Sharon, 'driving towards Knowle where Jason lives. Once again, and I'm not speaking as a member of the constabulary, it all seems speculative based on suspicion.'

'We have to do something,' pleaded Sally. 'How would we feel if we did nothing and later discovered that he had been continuing to kill patients for the last four-and-a-half years and that there were more premature deaths still to come?' Sally became very emotional and began to cry.

Sharon stood up, grabbed a tissue from a box on her desk and moved over to the sofa, where she crouched down beside Sally, handed her the tissue and put her arm around her. 'We *will* do something, Sally. Don't be upset. We also need to consider what the consequences would be if we made a false accusation. That would be devastating on so many levels.'

When Sally had composed herself once more, Sharon returned to her chair and clasped her hands together with interlinked fingers. After a few minutes deep in thought – though Greg suspected it was in prayer – Sharon came up with a suggestion.

'I think we should try and find out more about Jason before we do anything else. If he is as awful as this suggests, this could put us all in danger. If he is innocent, we will have saved ourselves embarrassment, and him, notoriety.'

'How?' asked Greg.

'How about,' Sharon put on a theatrical tone, 'An Evening with the Vicar.'

'A what?'

'An invitation to spend time with me, and my husband, in the company of other parishioners.'

'Did you just make that up?'

'Yes, actually.'

'When would this take place?'

'Are you free on Saturday?'

Greg and Sally looked at each other quizzically.

'I don't see why not,' said Greg, 'though I'm at work during the day.'

'Right then. Leave it to me. If I can get Jason to come, I'll let you know and we'll have a barbeque in our garden. Simon is king of the barbeque. He'll love it and the weather forecast is good for the next few days. Summer - at last.'

Sally, her eyes still red, spoke timidly. 'I have to admit I'm quite nervous, but if you think....'

'Don't worry, Sally. We have about forty-five hours to prepare.'

'That's what I'm nervous about.'

Friday 1st June

32

Fairwater and Hemmsworth, Funeral Directors, was established in 1936. The company had always prided itself in caring for the distinguished members of society. One of the ways they achieved this was by charging more than others. This meant that they could provide a very personal package for their clients and would go out of their way to provide a service that was far superior to those who considered themselves to be competitors.

The Greyson family had engaged them several times over the years, most notably for the former Lady Patience Greyson, the widow of Colonel Sir Timothy Henry Greyson Bt. in 1977. It was their privilege to organise the funeral arrangements for Sir Andrew James Greyson 4th Baronet of Knowle who had died at his Kensington home on the 25th May.

His widow, Katherine, and his son, the now Sir Christopher Edward Greyson 5th Baronet of Knowle, had followed Andrew's wishes to have a family funeral in St Mary Abbots Parish Church. The grand building was one of Sir George Gilbert Scott's final and greatest architectural works. Famous past parishioners included William

Wilberforce, Beatrix Potter, Isambard Kingdom Brunel and Sir Isaac Newton. The service took place on Thursday 31st May. A memorial service was to take place in a few weeks' time.

The cortège left the Greyson's home at 9am and travelled north via the M1 and M6 to Stafford. Family members had their lunch at The Manor House Hotel, where they were to stay overnight. Afterwards, the cortège slowed to a respectful pace along the country roads leading to Knowle.

They arrived, on schedule, at one-twenty-five. The Reverend Sharon Curtis, in her robes topped with a purple stole, was standing at the kerbside to welcome them. Mr Charles Clayton-Smith, the Funeral Director on this occasion, dressed in morning suit with a top hat, quickly introduced himself.

Eleven members of the Greyson family had made the journey and waited on the pavement while Andrew's coffin was taken from the hearse. Sharon introduced herself to the mourners and explained what would happen next, aware that some of them knew the procedure better than she did.

When they were ready, the coffin was shouldered by Sir Christopher, his uncle, his brother and his cousin for the short distance into the churchyard and to the entrance of the Greyson Crypt.

A few of the locals were present out of duty, respect or curiosity. For Bob White and Joyce Shilton, the churchwardens, it was the former. Others were standing at a respectful distance under the beech trees by the boundary wall, next to an eight-foot wooden cross. It had been put up for Holy Week and Easter some years previously, but had never been removed.

Much to everyone's relief, the weather was warm and dry, so those present were able to stand for the brief service. Sharon had spent nearly an hour that morning going over the words of the service even though it would last no more than six minutes. She had had to change a few of the words normally used for burials, as this would be in a crypt and not in a grave.

The end of the service was marked by a Blessing.

Mr Clayton-Smith took over from Sharon as he directed and aided his assistants and the bearers, in the tricky maneuver to enter the crypt, make a right-hand turn, descend the steps, and slide the coffin into the next available chamber.

Sharon had only spoken to Katherine on the phone before this occasion, so she took the opportunity to speak with her. Katherine told her that the family would be taking a look at the remains of Knowle Hall before they left the village as some of the younger members had never visited and wanted to see where the family had once lived.

The men emerged from the crypt and everyone from the cortège returned to their cars. When everyone had taken their seats and the funeral director had closed their doors and taken his seat, the cars slid away.

A local builder, Keith Watson, had been engaged to brick up the chamber as soon as the family had left. He appeared right on cue. Bob was on hand to supervise and lock the door immediately afterwards.

Sharon entered the church by the vestry door. She completed the entry in the Service Register that was kept on the top of the vestment cupboard. She then rummaged through the registers and record books in the safe to find the Crypt Record Book and completed entry number 11 directly under the previous entry from 1977 of Lady Patience Greyson.

She scanned the entries above. One of the entries saddened her. It recorded the burial of Juliet Halifax, the daughter of Sir Thomas Montague Greyson. She had died at childbirth along with the child she bore. They had been laid to rest together in the crypt.

With everything completed and her robes placed in her case, she left for home. She was relieved that it was over and that it had passed without a hitch. It would be an experience she could remember and recount for many years to come.

-o0o-

Back at The Vicarage, Sharon poured herself a glass of blackcurrant and apple squash. She carried it through to her study. Leaning back in her office chair, she closed her eyes and thought about her idea of hosting 'An Evening with the Vicar.'

Simon was quite amenable to the idea and had agreed to sort out the barbeque. They would buy the food needed that evening during their regular weekly Friday supermarket shop.

Importantly, Doctor Jason, responding to a message

left for him at the Cambridge Road Surgery, had said he would check his diary and get back to her as soon as possible, but had added that he didn't see any problem.

However, Sharon was concerned that it would appear too obvious to him if he realised that he was meeting with people who were looking into Rebecca's disappearance, and he was a suspect.

What she needed was an independent decoy, a parishioner who could be part of the evening with no agenda. She leaned forward, put her elbows on her desk and rested her head in her palms. Two minutes later she hadn't come up with a name, so she took a long drink of her squash.

Mrs Talbot – the village busy-body. Then again, NO.

Juliet Strange – churchwarden at Whittlebrugh. NO.

Darren and Clara Gibbons – the parents she had seen for a baptism preparation the evening before. Probably couldn't find a baby-sitter in time.

Think. Think. Think.

She took another gulp of squash hoping that it would help.

Denise what's-her-name? Denise had only been attending St Philip's for a few months. She had moved into the village after a divorce. On one occasion she had confided in Sharon that she had been granted a divorce from her husband of thirty-seven years. He had suddenly declared that he was in love with another man, and moved out to live with him!

Sharon flicked through some 'Welcome Cards' she kept in an index card box on her desk. She found the name she was looking for and took the card out. *YES.* Denise Morgan of 15 Braken Drive. She lifted the handset of her landline phone and entered the number - the number Denise had written on the card on her first visit to the church. The result of the brief conversation was that Denise was delighted to be asked and would be there the following evening. Job done!

Now time to finish preparations for the Sunday services.

-o0o-

Denise put her mobile down on the arm of her chair. The vicar had told her that there would be a few other people present and she wondered who they might be. Five months earlier, when she moved into Braken Drive, she didn't know anyone in the village. The purpose of her move to Whittlebrugh was to be nearer her daughter who lived in Stafford. Since then, she had met very few people. She had been warmly welcomed at the local church and had already been put on the rota for serving refreshments after the Sunday morning services.

Next, she thought about what she should wear. Should it be something casual or more formal. Now the weather had changed for the better, should she wear a summer dress? Probably the best way to be smart and casual at the same time.

She sprung out of her chair and rushed up the stairs to her bedroom and opened her wardrobe. Her move had demanded a major downsizing, so there were only a few summer dresses hanging on the rail. She pulled them out one at a time, stood in front of her full-length mirror, held them up in front of her to check what she would look like in each one.

Not one of them was what she wanted. She decided that this required a trip into town. She had discovered several charity shops on previous trips and she was sure she could find something appropriate in one of them. If not, she would try Stafford's High Street clothing establishments.

She planned to get up early in the morning, catch the Stafford bus, do some shopping, and call in to see her daughter, Tanya, while she was in there.

Saturday 2nd June

33

Simon spent the afternoon preparing the garden. The lawn had been mown and the edges trimmed. When he was satisfied with how it looked, he erected a pop-up gazebo, wheeled the bar-b-que from the rear of the garage, and dug out garden chairs and tables from the shed.

Sharon insisted that he hang some lights around even though Simon argued that, as it was nearly high summer, they would fulfill no practical purpose. That, according to Sharon, was not the purpose! He complied.

When he had done all that, he went into the kitchen and helped his wife prepare the salad and accompaniments.

On the dot of seven o'clock, the doorbell rang. Sharon opened the door and welcomed Denise. She was wearing a floral cotton dress with butterfly sleeves, looking spectacular for her age – so Tanya had told her when she was helping her with her makeup. Sharon led her through the living room's sliding patio doors onto the patio where Simon was tending to the smoldering charcoal bar-b-que.

Minutes later, Jason Edwards arrived in light-blue trousers and a blue check, open-neck shirt with button down collars. He was led on the same route and, like

Denise, was handed a glass of fruit punch.

Greg and Sally arrived just after five-past seven having walked the short distance from their home. Greg was wearing tan jeans and a rust-coloured shirt. Sally had chosen to wear an olive-green, ruffled-hem, tiered midi skirt with a light-green, embroidered blouse. Her hair was held back by a pretty, green, sparkly clip on each side - a souvenir from one of their holidays in Italy.

Simon, wearing a butcher's apron and a white chef's hat, had already started to grill the meat. Some foil-wrapped corn-on-the-cob was cooking on the edge of the grill.

Some country music, chosen by Simon, was playing gently in the background. Sharon introduced everyone. Greg and Sally hadn't met Jason before, so they were fascinated to see what he looked like. He was certainly tall, something over six-foot-two and had a neatly trimmed black beard. A pair of glasses sat on the bridge of his prominent nose. *Quite handsome for a murderer*, thought Sally.

Conversation began with the weather and its recent welcome transition. Next came the questions about their work and professions. Jason explained that he was a GP, then jested that that wasn't an invitation to ask him about their medical conditions, whether real or imagined. Greg told the others about his work as curator at the museum. Sally said that she worked at the Army barrack's, adding that she couldn't tell them what she did as she was *bound by the Official Secrets Act*. She went on, with a broad grin, to say that she always told people that because it was so much more impressive than if she had told them that she was actually a glorified secretary. Denise told them that she had recently begun working from home for a coffee capsule company as a telephone customer service adviser. Her actual work, she told them, involved helping callers who needed product information and order support.

By the time the introductions were fully made, Simon was ready with the meat and cobs. Sharon had set the chairs around a table loaded with the salads. She invited them to sit and help themselves to the food. Simon opened some wine bottles and filled their glasses.

Greg began a subtle interrogation of Jason. 'So Jason, is that your car in the drive?'

'If you mean the Mazda MX5 hard-top convertible. Yes, it's mine.'

'Very nice, I noticed the registration. It's only a couple of years old.'

'It is. I bought it with only five-thousand on the clock. I liked the slate-grey colour because I didn't want it to look too ostentatious.'

Greg had been worried that Jason didn't have a big car, but there was still hope. 'What did you have before this one?'

Jason seemed puzzled by the line of questions. He raised one eyebrow. 'Actually, it was a Jaguar XJ - a beast of a car. I'd had it for a few years, but I decided it was just too big for me.'

Food for thought.

Denise, who was sitting next to Jason, waited until

he had put a chunk of steak into his mouth before coyly saying, 'I really like the MX5.' Jason tried to smile and chew at the same time without great success.

'It seems to me,' said Simon, changing the subject, 'that you and Sharon have much in common in your professions.' No response. 'Well, Sharon is concerned for the soul and you, Jason, are concerned for the body.'

'And the mind.' retorted Jason.

'Of course. But both of you are trying to bring wholeness to your patients, stroke, parishioners, aren't you?'

'I guess.'

'And your faith must help you in your work, doesn't it?' asked Sharon.

'I'm not great at praying, but maybe.'

'To be honest, I'm not too great at praying either, but I do my best,' admitted Sharon.

'I think the secret to having a good life,' chuckled Denise, 'is to have a great coffee and a fine wine. In fact, any wine, and this is excellent.'

Remembering the conversation they had had in The Red Lion a few weeks earlier, Sally asked a loaded question of Sharon. 'What is the best part of your job, Sharon?'

'Ummm. Well, of course I love to do a wedding, but I think funerals are the most special because I have the privilege of helping people at the most difficult time of their lives. Spending time with the family of the deceased is one way I can help them deal with their loss. Getting them to speak about their loved one is cathartic. As I said, a privilege. Do you get that, Jason?'

'Sometimes. I much prefer it when my patients get better. Sadly, that is not always the case. I have to deal with death in a different way. I see many people at the end of their lives. I try to make their passing as easy as possible. *You* deal with the after effect: death.'

'I like to think I deal with the after effect: eternal life.'

'This is very morbid,' observed Denise. 'Can we talk about something else?'

'Holidays,' suggested Sally.

'Why not?' said Jason. 'Have you got any planned?'

'No,' Denise said happily, 'but I'm hoping to get away before long. I just need a companion.' To her disappointment, she received no offer.

'Greg and I had a great holiday earlier this year in the Dominican Republic. It was our first trip to the Caribbean. The country and the people were lovely.'

'I went to Cuba with my wife,' said Jason. 'That was spectacular, though not so much the wife bit.'

'You're married?' asked Denise transparently.

'Was married. It lasted seventeen-and-a-half years and ended in divorce. She couldn't cope with the hours I was working. Hey ho!'

'Oh!' Denise didn't manage to hide her renewed optimism very well.

'Sharon and I are thinking of going on a river cruise in Europe. Nothing fixed yet. This summer we're taking a couple of weeks on the Devon Riviera, just outside Torquay. If the weather stays like this, we couldn't ask for anywhere nicer.'

'In the autumn Sally and I are hoping to go to Italy. We've been a few times, but we've yet to visit Sorrento and Pompeii.'

'That sounds amazing.' said Sharon brightly. 'Can we come?' Simon stared at her over the top of his glasses in a meaningful way. 'Not to worry. Maybe we'll go another year.'

It was starting to cool especially as the patio was shaded from the evening sun. Sharon and Simon cleared the main course from the table and replaced it with a fresh fruit salad and cream, pouring and whipped.

The sleuths were taken aback when Jason asked, 'How are you doing in your search to find out about Rebecca Stainton?'

Suddenly, they didn't know what to say.

34

Simon jumped up from the table. 'Anyone want a top up?' he asked as he grabbed a wine bottle.

'Not for me,' said Jason. 'I'm driving.'

'I will,' said Denise with enthusiasm. 'I'm not driving. I'll have to walk home.' It was a kind of request, but once again, it failed.

'Yes please,' said Sally.

Greg was quick to accept. 'And me.'

When Simon had sat down once more, Sally attempted a reply. 'Well, Jason, you asked how our search for Rebecca is going. To be perfectly honest, we've been at it for a few weeks and, sad to say, there's nothing concrete yet.'

'Oh,' said Denise, rather surprised. 'So, you're the ones. I've heard about this. In fact, Sharon told us about it at the service a few weeks ago. I even took a pink bow home and put it on a bush by my front gate.'

'Thank you for that. As I say, we've not achieved much, but we're not giving up yet. The other day we were lent some photographs of her. They were probably the last ever taken of her. It was Boxing Day on The Green in Knowle.'

'I was there,' admitted Jason. 'Marigold Cottage is just around the corner.'

'Don't get the wrong idea,' informed Sharon to the others. 'Marigold Cottage is only a cottage by name. It's actually a grand house.'

'And it's a very fine house,' Jason acknowledged.

'Come to think of it,' said Greg weakly, 'I think you were in one of the pictures. I thought I'd seen you somewhere before. Must have been from that photo.'

'Yes. It must have been one of the last times I saw Rebecca. I knew her from The Oaks. I went away for a while in the new year and when I arrived home everyone seemed to be looking for her.'

'Did you? Well, you missed quite a frenzy. It was very cold and some of us searched into the night. A great tragedy.'

'Yes. Very sad. Look I'm sorry to be a bore, but I really must be getting off.' He stood up. 'Thank you so much for this evening. It's been very pleasant.'

'I'll have to go as well,' said Denise. 'I want to get back to my home in Braken Drive before it's dark. I don't like walking alone at this time of night.'

'I'll give you a lift if you like.'

'Oh really? That's very kind of you.' She was clearly delighted with the invitation. 'Are you sure it's not putting you to too much trouble?'

'Not at all.'

Simon stood and led them to the front door. He watched as Jason climbed into the car. He saw Denise's face as she climbed into the passenger seat. She was beaming.

'Well, what did you make of that?' asked Sharon.

'I'm not sure.' Greg cradled his wine glass. 'Is a Jaguar XJ a *big* car? He said he went away, but how do we really know if he wasn't back until *after* Rebecca went missing.'

'It's very hard, isn't it?' Sally continued, 'He seems such a nice man. I didn't expect him to volunteer so much. Was he genuine or was he being devious? I'm stumped.'

Simon leaned forward. 'One thing you could do, if you don't mind me suggesting it.'

'Go ahead.'

'Didn't you find out about the description of the car from some boys?'

'Yes.'

'Then show them a picture of a Jaguar XJ and ask them if the car they saw was like that.'

'Good idea,' said Sally. 'Thank you. We can do that. Do you know where the Groves live?'

'I can find that out for you,' said Sharon as she stood and made her way to her study. She returned a few minutes later holding a piece of paper. She handed it to Greg. 'Here you go.'

'Thanks. Now, can we help you to clear up?'

'No, we can do that,' said Sharon.

'Yes please,' corrected Simon. 'That would be great. Then we can get to bed before midnight. Sharon's up early tomorrow. It's a Sunday.'

-o0o-

It was still light and it was still quite warm as Greg

and Sally made their way home up Church Road. They walked hand-in-hand without speaking. They certainly felt that they knew Doctor Jason Edwards somewhat better having met him. *Was he a murderer? Was he a mass murderer?*

When they arrived back at number 62, Greg went straight to his computer and Googled pictures of the Jaguar XJ, found one and printed it off. He showed it to Sally. 'This should do the job. This should nail him.'

'Tomorrow will tell. Come on. I'm ready to climb Wooden Hill and slip down Sheet Lane.'

'I'm following.'

Sunday 3rd June

35

Sharon's first service was at Knowle, as usual, except on the fifth Sunday of the month when it was at Caulston. It only occurred about four times a year.

She looked at the congregation as she took her place at the front, and counted them. Today there were more than usual. It was boosted by the attendance of Sir Christopher and Lady Joanna Greyson. She was aware that he was now the Patron of the parish and would hold that responsibility when it came to appointing her successor. Altogether there were thirteen present in the church, including herself.

The sermon she had written was based on verses from Mark chapter 3. It was all about, she told them, doing good even when the time seemed inappropriate. 'Don't put off doing good whenever and wherever that might be. Jesus healed the man with the shriveled hand when it was the Sabbath - when it was supposed to be a day of rest. He told his critics, "Which is lawful on the Sabbath: to do good or to do evil, to save life or to kill?" So, today,' she concluded, 'with God's help, do your best to do good.'

At the end of the service, she made her way to the door and spoke to people as they left. The Greysons held back until everyone else, other than the ones who were finishing their duties in the vestry, had gone.

'May I steal a few minutes of your time?' asked Sir Christopher.

Sharon checked her watch knowing that the service at Whittlebrugh was due to begin in a short time. 'I only have a few minutes, but carry on.'

'It's about the crypt.'

'Is everything alright?'

'Frankly, Vicar, I'm not sure. You see, I was twenty-two when my grandmother, Patience, died and was placed in our crypt. I remember it vividly. On Friday I carried my father into the crypt and we laid him in the next available chamber: the fifth on the second row.'

'Right?' Sharon said, with concern in her voice at what might follow.

'I've been worrying about this since then.'

'He couldn't sleep for the last two nights,' added Lady Joanna.

'The thing is...' he drew a breath. '...I think Father should have been put in the fourth chamber.'

'I completed the Crypt Record Book,' said Sharon defensively, 'and Sir Andrew is entry number 11.'

'Exactly. Seven on the top row and the fourth on the second row. Father is in the twelfth chamber. Who is in the eleventh?'

Sharon was shocked to the point of being speechless. She thought quickly. 'Look, that is bizarre, but I must go for the service at Whittlebrugh. Can we speak later?'

'Of course,' replied Sir Christopher graciously. 'We

won't be going home until later on today.'

'May I call you?'

'Of course.' He pulled a card from his wallet and handed it to her. 'My mobile number's on there. Call me when you can.'

'I will, I promise, but excuse me for now.' She turned and rushed back to the vestry to collect her things before racing down the lane to Whittlebrugh – still wearing her robes.

-o0o-

The address Sharon had written on the paper for Brandon and Ryan Groves, was in Daisy Close, just a short distance from their home. At ten-thirty, just as Sharon was concluding the service at Knowle, they set off to walk to Daisy Close.

The house they wanted had a pocket handkerchief sized lawn at the front. A pink bow was tied to the door knocker. Greg knocked and Mrs Groves answered it. 'Hello again, Mrs Groves,' said Greg. 'May I introduce my wife, Sally.'

'Hi. How can I help?'

'We're wondering if we might ask your boys another question about the car they saw on the evening Rebecca went missing?'

'I guess so. Come in. The boys are playing on the trampoline. I'll call them in.'

She led them into the front room and invited them to sit. A large TV was sitting in the corner and game machine controllers were lying on the top of the TV stand.

Brandon and Ryan came in breathlessly. 'Hello again, boys.' Greg and Sally gave them big smiles.

'Hiya,' was their instinctive response. Their mother stood behind them, watching.

'Do you remember that we talked at school about Mrs Stainton and the fact that you saw her the evening she went missing?

'Oh yes, we remember,' said Brandon boldly.

'Good, well this is my wife, Sally.' He held up a folded piece of paper that he'd been carrying. 'I have a picture here that I want to show you. It's of a *big* car. I want you to tell me, if you can remember, if this is anything like the car you saw that day. Okay?'

'Cool!'

'Here it is.' He unfolded the paper and showed them the picture he had found of a Jaguar XJ.'

'No,' said Ryan. He twisted and looked up at his mother. 'Can I go now?'

'Sure.' Off he went.

Greg addressed Brendon. 'You agree with your brother?'

'Yes, I do.'

'How is this wrong?'

'That's a Jaguar. The car we saw wasn't a saloon. It was an SUV.'

The adults were quite surprised at Brandon's precise reply.

'And,' he continued, 'I'm pretty sure it was bright blue.'

'That's been really helpful.' said Sally genially 'Thank you Brandon.'

'Is that all?'

'Yes, thank you,' said Greg. Brandon raced out of the room as he and Sally stood to leave. 'Thank *you*, Mrs Groves. Your boys have been amazing.'

They returned to their home, both surprised and perplexed. 'Where do we go from here?' asked Greg.

'I guess we start looking for a bright blue SUV.'

36

At one-minute-past-twelve Greg's phone rang. He was sitting in a garden chair admiring his garden and watching Debbie chase butterflies as they flitted around the flower beds. He checked the screen and was surprised to see that it was Sharon.

'Hello, Sharon. I thought you would still be taking a service.'

'I was, but I had my mind on something very different. I suspect some of the congregation thought I must have had a bit too much of the Communion wine. I had to call you as soon as the service finished.'

'Ha ha. What's the hurry?'

'I think I may have found where Rebecca is.'

'Hold on a tick.' Greg signalled to Sally who was standing by the open kitchen door. She had come there on hearing the ringtone of Greg's phone. She came over to him and he turned on the speaker so she could hear. 'Sally's here now. Go ahead.'

'I was with Sir Christopher earlier this morning. We put his father in the crypt on Friday. Anyway, he thinks there is an extra, unexplained chamber bricked up in the Greyson crypt, one that isn't accounted for. What's the chance it might be where Rebecca is?'

'Really?'

'Really. We need to find out.'

'How on earth can we do that?'

'We need to take a look.'

'I have no idea what the crypt is like. What would we do?'

'Take some bricks out I suppose.'

'That sounds a bit spooky.'

'Dead people can't hurt you.'

'Physically? Perhaps not. Most likely to give me some horrendous nightmares though.'

'We need to do this, and do it soon.'

'Today?'

'Yes. Wait a minute. I've just had an idea.'

'What?'

'I've got to make another call. I'll call you back. Bye.'

Sally was open-mouthed. 'Are we going to open a grave?'

'I don't know. We'll just have to wait and see.'

'Let's grab a bite to eat just in case Sharon wants us to go straight away. She sounded in a hurry.'

'Good plan.'

They were just starting to eat when Greg's phone rang once more.

'It's me again. I've just spoken to Keith Watson, the builder who bricked up Sir Christopher yesterday. He lives in Knowle and is willing to come and help us. If we need to brick this chamber up again, he'll do that as well.'

'When?'

'Straight away. Can you come?'

'Hold on.' Greg checked with Sally. 'Yes, we'll be there as soon as possible. See you at Knowle Church.'

'Thanks. Bye.'

-o0o-

When they arrived, Sharon was waiting by the open crypt door with Simon. Greg quickly related the information they had found out from the Groves' boys about the car - the bright blue SUV.

She took that in, and then went on to explain that Keith, the builder, was already in the crypt with a battery-powered work lamp. 'Follow me, but be careful on the stairs,' she warned.'

They tentatively made their way down. It was surprisingly cold after the warmth at ground level. Keith had a bag of tools out of which he fished a cold chisel and lump hammer. 'Okay?' he said, 'Where do I start?'

Sharon pointed at the middle chamber on the second row. 'That one.'

Keith examined it. 'These bricks aren't so old. They look much like the ones we used when we put up the houses at Glebelands. That was about four years ago. Is that significant?'

'Maybe.'

'Look,' he leant down and grabbed an endoscope from his bag and linked it to his mobile phone. 'We don't have to make much of a hole. This little beauty will do the rest for us. I can push it through a small hole and we can see what's in there.'

'Perfect.'

'Here goes. Stand back.'

Keith donned safety goggles, selected a half brick and started hammering away at the mortar surrounding it. 'Not very well done,' he muttered.

The noise was really loud in the small space and the others, intuitively, put their hands over their ears. It took several minutes as he chipped at the mortar and the brick itself. Eventually, with just a little left, he reversed the hammer and knocked the remainder into the void with the end of the wooden handle.

A smell permeated the crypt like nothing any of them had experienced before. Keith pushed the endoscope though the hole. He held his mobile so that everyone, now crowding around, could see the image. The integral LEDs made it possible for them to see what was there for themselves. Sally let out a muted shriek.

Sharon spoke decisively. 'I think we've seen enough.'

At that moment the crypt door slammed shut. It made them all jump.

'What the...'

37

Simon ran up the stairs closely followed by Greg. He pushed the door. It wouldn't shift. He stepped back and barged at it. It still wouldn't budge. 'We're trapped,' he called out.

'Let's try together,' suggested Greg. They stepped back to the edge of the platform and, on the count of three, charged at the door. It still wouldn't move. Something significant was holding it in place.

'We need some help,' called Simon.

'I'll phone someone,' called back Sharon from the bottom of the stairs.

Sally was shaking. 'Who're going to call?'

'Ghost Busters,' drawled Keith.

'Not funny!'

'The nearest is probably Doctor Edwards. What do you think?'

'Go for it.' Sally was clearly distraught. 'Just get it done.'

Sharon stared at the screen. She had the surgery number stored, but not a personal number. Then she remembered that he had texted her with an acceptance to the bar-b-que. She went into the texts, found his, and rang him. 'Jason. This is Sharon Curtis. Are you at home?'

'Yes. What can I do for you?'

Sharon explained their predicament as briefly as she could.

'Hang on. I'm on my way.' Not that they could go anywhere.

True to his word, a few minutes later Jason was at the door. Sharon let out a deep sigh of relief when he called out to them. They heard noises and suddenly the door burst open. Welcome daylight flooding the entrance – for them, the exit.

Simon and Greg were first out, quickly followed by Sally and Sharon with Keith not far behind. Jason was standing a few feet away holding the eight-foot wooden cross upright.

Their puzzled looks were answered by him. 'This was jammed against the door, the base sunk into the ground. I can tell you that it was quite a challenge to move from *this* side. Are you all okay?'

Sally sat down on the grass. 'Just a little shaken,' she said. Strangely, she looked around and thought how pretty the daisies were!

'It's a good job he didn't just lock the door and throw the key away.' observed Simon.

'It's a good job I pocketed the key,' Sharon replied showing them the key she had pulled from her pocket. 'I had it with me the whole time'.

'The big question is this,' said Greg. 'Who would have blocked the door with us inside?'

'And why?' added Sharon.

Sally looked up at the others. 'Surely it must have been someone who knew what we were doing and wanted to stop us from getting out. Well, at least getting out quickly.' Her mind was racing. 'Someone who needed time to get away before we escaped. Did anyone else know we were going to be here?'

Sharon pondered briefly, not sure of the consequences of what she was about to say. 'I did call Bob and tell him we would be investigating a mystery in the crypt, but I can't imagine he would do something like this. It doesn't make sense.'

'We can check that out. Sally and I can pop 'round to his house.'

'I can call him,' offered Sharon.

'Do it.'

Sharon called Bob's mobile. It went to voicemail. She then called his landline. That one wasn't answered either.

'That's settled then. Sally and I'll go to his home. It'll only take a few minutes.' He pulled Sally up from the ground and led her to their car. They were soon out of sight.

-o0o-

Greg knocked on the door and rang the bell of Number 14 Prospect Terraces. There was no answer. He tried to find his way down the side of the house via a covered passageway. A six-foot high gate blocked his way. It was locked or bolted. He returned to the front door. Sally was peering through the front bay window into the room they had sat in, enjoying tea and fairy cakes, a few weeks before. There was nothing unusual, other than she noticed that some of the family photographs had been removed from the mantelpiece.

Greg began knocking on the door again in frustration. The neighbour from Number 16 came out to find out what was happening. 'They've gone away,' she said.

'When?' asked Greg.

'They left less than half-an-hour ago in their car.'

'As a matter of interest,' asked Sally pointedly, 'do you know what kind of car Bob and Joan have?'

'It's a white... Ummm... Sportage something or other.'

'Kia Sportage?'

'Yeah. That sounds right.'

'Not bright blue then?'

'No, though I seem to remember they changed a few years ago from one that was blue, bright blue. Their new car looks a lot sleeker.'

Greg and Sally looked at each other incredulously. *Could Bob have been the person last seen with Rebecca?*

'You don't happen to know *where* they were headed do you?'

'Sorry, no. I did notice them taking bags to the car so they're probably taking their caravan away for a spell.'

'Thank you. You've been more helpful than you can imagine.' Greg and Sally rushed back to their car and returned to the church.

The other four were still there standing near the crypt door.

'You'll never guess what?' said Greg excitedly. 'Bob

and Joan left a short time ago in their Kia Sportage. That's a *big* car, an *SUV*.'

Keith and Jason looked puzzled.

Sharon explained Jason's presence. 'While you were gone, Doctor Edwards here, took a look into the void with Keith's help.' Then turning to Jason, 'Didn't you?'

'I did. I'm pretty sure that the body down there is of a young woman. I'm not a pathologist, but I think she's been in there for a few years. You may just have found Rebecca Stainton.'

'Now is the time to call the police,' declared Sharon. 'Agreed?' Five heads nodded agreement. She took her mobile and called 9 9 9.

The call was quite short and to the point. The police would be dispatched immediately.

Sally was a step ahead. 'The next question is, where would Bob and Joan go?'

38

An idea leapt into Greg's head. 'Excuse us,' he said, 'we have somewhere to be. We'll keep in touch. Oh, and we'll speak to David and her parents. We promised to let them know as soon as we were sure of anything, and I'm sure.' Sally was bewildered. Nevertheless, she followed Greg to the car.

Greg drove back towards Whittlebrugh with a lot on his mind. 'Where are we going?' Sally asked.

'In a minute,' he replied. They passed the field of rapeseed where the bomb had been detonated. The scar from the excavation and explosion could still be seen. However, the bright yellow of the rapeseed flowers had gone, leaving the maturing green crop.

They crossed the canal bridge. 'Come on, Greg, where are we going?' begged Sally.

'We're going on a road trip. First, we need to go home and pick up a few things. We'll have to take Debbie with us 'cos we don't have time to take her to Mark's.'

'Where?'

'Trust me - you'll see.'

Once they arrived home Greg persuaded Sally to put together a few things just in case. He hurried her along and within ten minutes they were back in their Dacia Duster.

Sally was determined to know what Greg was planning. 'You have to tell me now.'

He was heading for the M6 motorway. 'I think we may be an hour behind Bob and Joan. Possibly more, but maybe quite a bit less, assuming they've had to collect their caravan from a storage site.'

'Where do you think they're headed?'

'Chetmouth. Remember? They told us it was their favourite place.'

'You sure?'

'I can't be one-hundred-percent sure, but it's worth a go.'

When he entered the motorway, he accelerated to seventy. 'Look out for a caravan being towed by a white Kia Sportage.'

'Why do you think they will have their caravan?'

'I think they'll try to hide somewhere while they figure out what to do next.'

'We *are* sure that Bob's the culprit, aren't we?'

'You tell me. Tell me what links him with what we've learnt so far?'

'Okay,' she replied reflectively. 'We found out that Rebecca was last seen on the fifteenth of January by the Groves' boys, getting into a *big* car. When we spoke to Brandon earlier, he described the car as a bright blue SUV. Bob and Joan's neighbour told us that they used to have a bright-blue Kia Sportage.'

'Next?'

'We found Rebecca in the Greyson Crypt to which Bob had access.'

'Yes, he could have easily taken the key from the safe and then thrown it into the canal where Cliff found it. That was a lucky and timely find.'

'Sharon had told him that we were going to be at the crypt. He was probably the only other person who knew that, so it's likely that he was the one who barricaded us in.'

Sally pointed forward. 'There's a caravan up ahead.'

'Got it.' Greg approached and then slowed down to just over sixty to overtake. The caravan was being pulled by a Volvo. 'Not this one,' he said, and sped up again.

'What I don't understand,' said Sally, 'is what his motive could have been. Everyone seemed to like and respect Rebecca.'

'I agree. Bob doesn't appear to be the murdering type.'

Greg transferred onto the M5 at the Ray Hall Triangle. He was keeping up a good speed and had overtaken several caravans already, but not the one they were looking for.

-oOo-

Doctor Jason felt it was now his responsibility to stay at the crypt. He was aware that he might now be called as a witness should there be a court case - a very likely outcome in his opinion.

Keith had packed his bag with the endoscope and tools and left, leaving behind the LED lamp at Sharon's request.

'You know, Jason,' said Sharon jovially, 'until this

morning you were on our list of suspects.'

'Really!'

'We think Rebecca was keeping an eye on you and was going to expose you as a mass murderer.'

'A what?' he exclaimed.

'We think, she thought that patients were dying suspiciously quickly at The Oaks on the occasions when you attended them.'

'That's absurd. I know she was a tender soul, but to accuse me of such a thing is quite scandalous.'

'It certainly would have been a scandal.'

'One that I would have defended vigorously. What made you change your mind?'

'Your car. Witnesses have come to light who saw Rebecca getting into a bright blue SUV on that evening. We saw your Mazda when you came to The Vicarage yesterday. You told us about your Jaguar. Neither one came anywhere near the description of a bright blue SUV.'

'Another thing,' added Simon, 'I don't think you'd have come to get us out of the crypt if it was you who blocked us in.'

'Damn right. Anyway, I was in New York when Rebecca disappeared. I caught news of it on *BBC World News*. I flew home the Saturday afterwards and found the place buzzing.'

Sharon continued. 'That would have been quite a trick - long distance abduction. What were you doing there?'

'I wanted to visit Ground Zero - the 9/11 Memorial

and Museum. A friend had told me it was worth a visit. Let me tell you, I didn't realise what a remarkable, somber and disturbing experience it would be. I thought I'd be there for an hour. I was there for over three-and-a-half hours.'

'Wow! Oh hang on, I need to call Sir Christopher. He ought to be here.'

The three of them turned around as blue lights swept the scene.

-o0o-

Greg had suggested that they should drive through the motorway service areas and check if Bob and Joan's car and caravan were parked up. The first one he pulled into was Moto Frankley, south-west of Birmingham.

'Let's call David while we're here, shall we?'

'Good idea. I'll let you do the talking.'

Greg found his number and the line connected. 'David. It's Greg Williams. Can we talk?'

'Of course.'

'Are you sitting down?'

'You've found Rebecca, haven't you?' he said anxiously.

'We think we have, though I'm sure that her body will have to be officially identified before we can be certain.'

'Where?' His voice was quivering.

'In the crypt of the church at Knowle.'

'Oh! How did she die?'

'We have no idea. She was bricked up. An endoscope was used to take a peek. It's now up to the authorities to do what's required.'

Greg could hear him breathing heavily. 'I'm coming down,' he said abruptly. 'I can be there in a couple of hours or so.'

'You won't be able to do anything.'

'I don't care. I need to be close.'

'We're not there at the moment – but, Sharon Curtis will be able to tell you all that we know, and perhaps more. I'll text you her mobile number. Okay?'

'Yes. Thanks.'

'Look, I'm sorry to bring you bad news.'

'It certainly is bad news, though it's actually better than no news. Thank you.'

'Take care, David. Don't rush. A few minutes extra won't change anything.'

'I won't. Thanks again.'

The line went dead. 'Now for Mr and Mrs Bailey. I think it's your turn. Okay?'

'Not really, but I'll have a go. Their number's in my phone anyway.' She dug it out of her bag. As usual it was at the bottom, and it was a big bag.

She made the call. She was about to give up after eleven rings when Robert answered with a greeting which also served as a question. 'Good afternoon?'

'Good afternoon. Mr Bailey, I presume. It's Sally Williams. We met in Whittlebrugh.'

'Ah, yes. You've taken up the challenge to find Rebecca. How's that going? Oh, hold on. There's someone calling me on my mobile.'

Sally could hear that a conversation was going on,

though she couldn't tell what was being said as it was so muffled. She guessed Robert had his hand over the mouthpiece. She waited for a few minutes before Robert came back on.

'Hello again Sally. I have a feeling you're just about to tell me that you think you've found the body of our daughter. That was David calling on my mobile. He's just leaving to drive down to Whittlebrugh.'

'You're quite right. Is there anything we can help you with?'

'You could tell me who killed her.'

'Actually, I can't. I suspect, though, that that will become clear very soon. Please be patient.'

'After four-and-a-half years, it looks as though I'll have to be.'

'I promise that, if I find out, I'll let you know at the first opportunity.'

'Well, thank you. I'm going to ring off now. I have to break this news to Mary.'

'Do give her our very best. We'll be in touch. Bye.'

Sally put her mobile back into her bag.

'That's all done.'

'How'd it go?'

'Alright considering.'

'Time to get back on the road. I have a feeling we still have a way to go. He started the engine and made his way back onto the motorway.

Little did they know that Bob and Joan were running scared some miles in front of them.

39

The miles flew by. Greg drove through the service area car parks at Strensham, Gloucestershire, Michaelwood, Gordano, Sedgemoor - where they stopped for a comfort break and fuel - Bridgewater and Taunton Dean. They had encountered dozens of caravans. Bob and Joan's was not to be found.

'They could have stopped somewhere off the motorway you know,' observed Sally.

'True. They could still be in front.'

'That's becoming less likely though, isn't it?'

'It is. We've been on the road for two-and-a-half hours and now I'm famished. The food we prepared for our lunch didn't go very far, did it?'

'No, but as we've come this far...'

'...we ought to carry on.'

'To where?'

'Not sure. We should try and find out where the caravan sites are around Chetmouth.'

'Keep going for now, there's still a small chance they're in front of us, after all we've spent some time in all of the service areas.'

'Next one is Cullompton. I'm pretty sure they won't

stop there 'cos it's so small, and that's the last one before Exeter and the turning for Chetmouth.'

'Chetmouth - the place we solved our first mystery together.'

'Seems an age ago now.'

'Hopefully we can wrap this one up there too.'

- o 0 o -

The first police car was soon joined by a second, and a third. Within the space of a couple of hours the village was awash with detectives and Scenes of Crime forensic officers. A tent had been erected across the entrance to the crypt and specialists were coming and going.

Graham Tetley, from the *Stafford Mail* had received a text message from Greg Williams. It didn't actually say who it was from, but it was obvious. He'd rushed out to Knowle, but was held back by a police cordon. As promised, he had passed on details to Ed, his colleague from *Reuters*. Strangely though, he couldn't find Ed's number for an hour or so!

Sir Christopher and Lady Joanna arrived and Sharon told them about Rebecca's disappearance and the likelihood that it was her body in the crypt.

At four o'clock Sharon asked if she could leave as she had an evening service at four-thirty. A DS from the Major Crimes Unit checked her contact details and gave her, and Simon, permission to leave. They still hadn't had any lunch.

- o 0 o -

At Taunton Bob had taken the exit towards the town. He knew from past experience that the supermarket fuel was far cheaper than at the motorway service areas. It didn't take them long and while he was filling the tank, Joan walked over to the store to buy some food. It was about to close, being Sunday, so she rushed around and grabbed what she needed. The bakery bread had sold out so she had to settle for a Warburton's 'Toastie'. With two full shopping bags, she walked back to the filling station.

She had the niggling feeling that someone was watching her. She knew well that it was only paranoia. She had experienced the same feeling over four years previously and it was scary. As the months had passed the feeling faded and she was able to get on with life. Now it was back with a vengeance. *Was it paranoia or was someone really watching this time?*

Bob was sitting in the driver's seat, waiting. She opened the rear door and placed the bags on the back seat before taking her place in the passenger seat. Bob started the engine. 'Not too far now, Love,' he said.

Bob was the practical one. He always had been. If there was a problem, he solved it. He was good with his hands and could do anything he put his mind to, except for making fairy cakes, which was definitely her strong point.

He had been zealous about St Saviour's for as long as she could remember. She sometimes thought he loved the church more than her. Well, he spent more time on church matters than the things *she* wanted to do. That wasn't strictly true. When they were in their caravan it was very different.

And here they were, off to their special place where

they would usually find some peace and quiet – their *happy place*.

She looked to the left. She could see the Wellington Monument on the top of the hill. She'd read somewhere that, at one-hundred-and-seventy-five feet, it was the tallest triangular obelisk in the world.

Wellington was a hero, and I'm a coward.

Her Waterloo defeat was on the fifteenth of January four years previously. It wasn't a battle, but the consequences were horrific. Now they were running away. In a way she hoped it would soon be over. In fact, the sooner the better.

-o0o-

Greg left the motorway at Exeter and started along the road towards Chetmouth. 'Let's assume they're behind us,' suggested Greg. 'If we can find a layby on the road towards Chetmouth, we can just watch and wait. Surely it can't take them more than five hours.'

'What about some food?'

'Maybe we can kill two birds with one stone.'

'How so?'

'Do you remember stopping at a pub along here. It was where I bumped into a car on purpose.'

'Oh yes.'

'Now what was it called? Oh, I know, *The Highwayman.* Keep a lookout. It can't be far away. We can grab some food and watch the traffic pass us. If they come this way, we'll see them.'

'You're the boss.'

He grinned at her. 'That makes a nice change.'

A few minutes later they pulled into the car park of *The Highwayman*. A painted 'A' board stated that there was a Public Bar, Beer Garden and a Restaurant with Takeaways available. At the bottom it stated: *Well behaved dogs are Welcome*. That was convenient for them. Greg parked his car facing the road. Sally volunteered him to find something for them to eat, while she watched for the Whites and their car and caravan outfit.

Having ordered, Greg fetched Debbie from the back of the car and took her for a walk in the very small dog exercise field, then put her back in the boot of the car. Altogether, it took twenty-five minutes for him to finally bring the food back.

'So, what have you brought us?' said Sally, sniffing the air.

'A speciality at The Highwayman. It's Baked Buffalo Chicken Wings with chips, of course, with a side of coleslaw.'

'To drink?'

'Cola. No sign of Bob and Joan?'

'Nope.'

They sat in the car with the windows down. The evening was going to be lovely. There were some puffy white clouds sliding across the azure sky.

They were well into their sticky chicken wings, eating them with their fingers, when Sally spotted a white vehicle approaching, towing a caravan. 'Is this them?' she said hopefully.

'It's a Kia.' They watched carefully. 'I think... yes, it's them.' He quickly passed his carton of unfinished wings and chips to Sally, fastened his belt, started the engine and swung back onto the road in pursuit.

'I *was* right,' he declared triumphantly.

40

David made his way through the upper part of Whittlebrugh village to The Vicarage. It was so familiar, though different at the same time. It brought back some happy and some sad memories of the parish he had left so suddenly and painfully.

In contrast, he was gob-smacked to see so many pink ribbons tied to gates, and doors, and bushes, and trees, and fences. They were everywhere.

He parked on the road-side outside his old home out of respect for the present residents, and ambled up the drive observing the shrubs. They appeared to have grown exponentially in the four years since he had left. He noticed that the windows had been replaced with UPVC frames.

He was about to knock when a car drew up behind him. He turned to see his successor, Sharon Curtis, climb out of the car wearing a black skirt, and a black shirt with a clerical collar. 'David, I presume,' she called. 'You are most welcome.'

'Thank you,' he answered. 'It does feel strange to be back.'

'Please come in.' She unlocked and opened the front door. I'm sure you will find this weird. Like, it's the familiar building with unfamiliar furniture.'

She led him into the lounge where Simon was watching TV. He grabbed the remote and turned off the TV before standing up to greet the man of whom he had heard so much. Sharon introduced them to each other.

'It's really nice to meet you at last. So sorry it's in these circumstances.' They shook hands. 'Please sit down. I'll put the kettle on while you settle down.' He backed out of the room.

David looked around. 'You've done a nice job in here,' he said graciously.

'That's very kind of you. You must be tired after your journey. Is there anything we can give you?'

'Thank you. I'll be alright. Really.

'So, I expect you want to know what we know about Rebecca.'

'Yes please.'

'Greg and Sally Williams have done an amazing job, talking to people, reviving memories etcetera. You've met them, haven't you? Serendipity played its part as well. Two local men went magnet fishing in the canal just by the Knowle Lane bridge and found a key. They took it to The Red Lion where it was added to Terry's collection on the beams. I expect you knew Terry.' He nodded in the affirmative.

'Then, Sir Andrew Greyson died and we discovered the Greyson Crypt key was missing. We found it at The Red Lion. Amazing, isn't it? Bit of a miracle really. Then on Friday, Sir Andrew was placed in the crypt and we discovered that a chamber was bricked up that wasn't recorded. So, earlier today we took a look, and that's when we discovered Rebecca. Well, we're pretty sure it's her.'

'Can I see her?'

'That's not up to me of course. The police have taken over. And anyway, after all this time, I'm not sure you would want to *see* her. Better to remember her as she was, a very lovely, sweet young lady, from all that I've heard.'

Simon entered the room and placed a tray on the coffee table. It was laden with masses of finger food. 'I hope you will join us,' he said. 'We haven't had our supper yet. For that matter, we didn't have any lunch either.' Without waiting for an answer, he handed out plates and disappeared again to fetch cups of tea.

'This is very kind. Thank you. It seems rude not to.'

'Our pleasure.' They filled their plates and sat back to eat.

'Do you know who killed her?'

'Not yet determined. However, and you might find this as hard to believe as I do, Greg and Sally have gone off on a mission to find Bob and Joan White.'

'Whaaaat? That can't be. They are as sweet as sugar.'

'I'm afraid to say, we'll have to wait and see.'

Simon re-entered with another tray on which he had cups of tea and a stack of cakes. 'This should keep us going.'

David ignored Simon as he was clearly stunned by the suggestion. He put his plate down. 'But why?'

'No idea. I'm sure it'll come out in the end.'

'Goodness me!'

A few minutes passed as David let it soak in. Sharon and Simon left him to his thoughts.

'Sorry,' he began, 'it's simply mind-blowing.'

'My apologies as well,' said Sharon. 'We didn't ask if you have somewhere to stay. You would be most welcome to stay in the guest room.'

'No. Again, that's very kind. Philip and Patricia Jones are putting me up.'

'Perfect. Please remember that if there is *anything* we can do....'

'You've done so much already. This is amazing,' he said as he picked his plate up and continued to eat.

-o0o-

Bob was driving down the road confidently. It was clear to Greg that he was familiar with the road and had years of experience in towing caravans. Bob drove past the turning on the right which would have taken him into the town, and continued for a mile or so along the coastal road. Unaware of the car following him purposefully, he slowed down and turned right into a narrow lane. Greg followed cautiously.

After about fifty yards Greg stopped to watch Bob turn into a field. They followed through the entrance stealthily. Caravans and tents were scattered around. Most were on the far side, lined up against a sheep wire fence. Suddenly he knew where he was. 'Sal, do you know where we are?'

'No. Should I?'

'Don't you remember that I brought you here when

Mark was about four years old. We were camping and the wind rose, shaking the tent like anything.'

'Oh. Don't remind me. I do remember being very frightened that the tent might be blown over the cliff into the sea.'

'That's it. We never went camping again, did we?'

'No, thank goodness.'

'Well, here we are once more. Doesn't look so bad in this weather, does it? And I see they've built a toilet block. Much better.'

'What do we do now?' asked Sally.

'Wait until they've set up and can't do a runner, then we'll go and have a word with them.'

'Won't that be dangerous?'

'I don't think so. If it were us, I think we'd be scared sick. I'm sure that's how they feel.'

'We can't stay here.'

'Why not. If someone comes, we'll move.'

They waited. While they waited, they finished off their Baked Buffalo Chicken Wings with chips and coleslaw, and drank the Coke. Despite being cold, it was altogether very tasty.

As they ate, they watched as Bob and Joan unhitched their van and, using a remote-control device, twisted the caravan so that the front was facing the sea. Bob lowered the steadies and moved his car to left-hand side - adjacent to the van door.

After about twenty minutes, Greg and Sally agreed it was time to confront the Whites. Greg drove across the field and stopped his car immediately behind the Kia, leaving no chance of it being driven away other than over the clifftop.

Bob and Joan saw them as they approached the door. Bob got up from his seat and opened the door. 'You better come in,' he said dejectedly.

41

David left The Vicarage to go to Philip and Patricia's home. However, he couldn't resist driving to Knowle Church to see the place where his dear wife had been hidden for so long. It was seven-twenty when he arrived.

He was mildly surprised to find that there was a small crowd assembled across the road from the church. Police vehicles were parked outside the churchyard and there was quite a lot of activity going on. He guessed that, if he stopped, he would become the focus of conversation and questions, and he didn't think he could face that, so he continued straight past.

When he arrived at the Joneses' house, he was welcomed warmly. Patricia gave him a long, comforting hug. It felt lovely, but left him quite emotional.

He was offered supper, which he declined, accepting instead, a dram of Scotch. He downed in one go.

His hosts chose to let him relax rather than engage him in conversation. It suited him well. After a while he closed his eyes and drifted off.

-oOo-

Joan was sitting at the table with a plate of half-eaten

supermarket sandwiches in front of her. She and Bob were wearing sweaters with open, moss-green gilets. Bob had been sitting opposite Joan. He moved his plate of sandwiches onto the kitchen worktop and invited Greg and Sally to sit on that side of the table. He took the vacant place next to his wife. Sally shuffled along the cushioned bench and Greg took his place next to her.

The view from the window was spectacular. The sky was blue and the evening sun was giving an orange glow. There were, perhaps, half-a-dozen ships way out, with smaller craft, including yachts, nearer to the coast.

The caravan was pitched close to the fence. On the other side of the fence there was a ribbon of grass, some ten metres wide, along which walkers were traversing the long-distance South-West Coastal Path. The site's own access gate to the coastal path was, conveniently, just a few metres to the right of where the caravan stood. Beyond the grass the land fell away into the sea.

Greg had heard about a recent dramatic landslide further along the coast. That one had taken hundreds of tons of cliff into the waves. He wondered if they were safe so close to the edge. *Probably.*

'I think you ought to start from the beginning,' suggested Sally.

'I think that would be best,' agreed Joan. She looked at Bob who took the hint.

'On Wednesday January fifteenth I saw Rebecca walking on Church Road on her way home. I offered to give her a lift as I had something I wanted to discuss with her.

She gladly jumped in. I drove onto Knowle Lane. She began to be a little distressed, perhaps thinking I was up to no good, so I pulled into the layby near the canal bridge. She jumped out, so I got out to assure her that I wanted her help. I told her that Joan and I wanted to ask her to be an advocate for us and that we could explain it all better at home. In the end she agreed and climbed back in. I took her straight to Prospect Terraces.

'She happily came inside having seen Joan at the window. We sat her down and Joan plied her with her fairy cakes and tea.'

'What was this thing you wanted her help with?' asked Sally firmly.

'I was coming to that. We had heard that the Diocese had put forward a plan to close St Saviour's Church. St Saviour's is the heart of our little village, even more so now that The Bell has closed. It was rumored that David was in agreement. The intention was that the church would only be open for services at the major festivals, and that's all. Our church has served this community for generations. We manage to keep it in good order and do all the repairs aided by the generosity of the Greyson family.'

'I thought,' butted in Joan, 'that they would close our church and make the Whittlebrugh vicar take on another, bigger parish nearby.'

'So, how could Rebecca have helped?' Greg this time.

Bob answered. 'It's common knowledge that women are the really powerful ones, despite what *they* say. We wanted Rebecca to persuade David to fight for us and save

St Saviour's. That's what we asked her to do.'

'The very next thing,' Joan said animatedly, 'was that she stood up and laughed at us.'

'Joan stood up too and blocked Rebecca's way to the door. She said something about us being silly. She was sneering. She tried to squeeze past. Then Joan pushed back, not hard mind you, and she tripped backwards over the coffee table. I leapt up. As I did, I watched her fall. She looked petrified. I was too slow - far too slow.'

'It was horrible.'

'Her head hit the edge of our brick fireplace...'

'And she lay there - still.'

'We both bent down to try to bring her 'round, but there was nothing.'

'I felt for a pulse, but couldn't find one.'

'Blood was seeping from her head.'

'We lay her out on the rug and Bob tried CPR. He took a First Aid course a couple of years before, so he knew what he was doing.'

'After going at it for ages, I gave up. There was blood everywhere.'

'Then we panicked. What should we do? We'd killed the vicar's wife.'

'It seems silly now, but we sat down and finished our cups of tea and ate some cake.'

'Bob came up with a plan. He reckoned that if we hid her body somewhere it would never be found, we wouldn't be caught.'

'Yes, I knew the perfect place - the Greyson crypt.

No one ever goes in there except when a family member is put there, and that hadn't happened for thirty odd years. I actually thought it might never happen again as so many people choose cremation these days.

'We waited until it was dark and put Rebecca in the back of our car for the short trip to the church. She was wrapped up in the blood-soaked rug. I fetched the key from the safe and together we managed to get her down the stairs and into the next empty crypt chamber.'

Joan took up the account. 'We were still there when I received a call from David to tell us that Rebecca was missing, so Bob and I joined the search party. I felt so guilty, but I didn't want to go to prison, and I didn't want Bob to take the blame. After all, it was *me* who pushed her.'

'A few days later,' Bob continued, 'I filched some sand and bricks from the Glebelands building site. I had to buy some cement from the builders' merchant over in Stafford to mix up the mortar.'

'He went out in the middle of the night and was gone for an hour or so.'

'When I'd finished the job, I locked the door and decided to get rid of the key, so I drove down to the canal and tossed it in.'

Joan was eager to say something. 'Then you two started asking questions. Then Sharon wanted the key and Bob had to pretend he didn't know anything about it not being in the safe. It was frightening.'

'Not as frightening as it was for David and everyone else.' Sally was openly irate. 'You've acted as if you knew nothing for all this time. How cruel was that?'

Joan was defensive. 'It was an accident. We couldn't undo it. We laid her to rest in church. What more could we have done?'

'You could have told the truth. You could have spared David, her family and friends, years of worry, sadness, despair, anxiety, depression. The list goes on.'

A guilty silence followed.

Greg leaned forward coolly. 'You do realise that the time has come to come clean, don't you? If we leave you here, you'll soon be found by the police wherever you try to hide. This has to end now.'

'I accept that,' said Bob in resignation.

'I know,' agreed Joan. 'To be perfectly honest, I'm relieved.'

'What happens now?'

'I've been thinking about that. We happen to have an acquaintance who's a detective with the Devon and Cornwall Police. I think we might call him. I'm sure he'll do the right thing for you. Hold on. I'll step outside and give him a call. Okay?'

No one objected. A few minutes later he came back into the caravan. 'I called Peter Barnaby's number. It was automatically transferred to another number. Apparently, Peter's away. A DI, Ian Harris from Exeter, is going to come and see us here. We just have to wait until he arrives.'

'Excuse me,' said Joan, 'I need to fetch my handbag from the car.' Bob stood and she shuffled out.

She closed the caravan door behind her and they

watched as she walked in front of the caravan and headed straight for the costal path's access gate. She unfastened it and started through it. Bob, Greg and Sally looked at each other in horror. Greg led the way as they rushed out of the caravan.

42

Joan was walking towards the cliff edge. Greg raced through after her. Bob shouted, 'Joan, where are you going? Come back.'

She stopped and turned to look at them. Bob and Sally had stayed behind the fence.

'Joan, come back.' Greg said in a soothing way.

'I've got to do this.'

'This isn't the way. You have no idea how this will turn out.'

'I'll go to prison.'

'That's possible, but not certain.' Joan turned her head to look at the cliff top and, as she did, Greg took a short step towards her.

'I promise, we'll do all we can to help you. It was clearly an accident. They're bound to take that into consideration.' He caught movement in the corner of his eye and turned his head to the left to see a man and a woman approaching them along the coastal path. He raised his voice to a command. 'Stop.' Then gentler, 'Please stay there.' They obeyed as they comprehended the situation.

'Thank you.'

Bob called over to her. 'Joan, please come back. We

can work this out.'

'It's no good, my dear. I've lived with this for four-and -a-half years. I want it to be over.'

Greg saw a family coming from the other direction. A dog was running loose in front of them.

'We have a situation here,' he called. 'Please call your dog back and return the way you've come. This is no place for children.' They appeared startled, but did what he told them.

He turned his attention back to Joan. 'I have to do it,' she whimpered.

'Listen, Joan.' Greg's voice was quiet, barely audible to the others watching. 'I promise you this: If you *do* jump, you'll regret it as you fall. In those few seconds, you'll think of all the things and people you'll miss. You *will* find ways to cope for the future. If you jump it will be too late to change your mind. None of us want that.'

Joan was silent - thinking. Greg took another small step towards her.

'I don't know.' Another hushed moment. Greg became aware of the sound of the sea, and seagulls squawking in the distance.

'Come back to me, Joan. It's going to be alright, I promise you.'

She looked directly at him and took a step towards him. Over his shoulder she caught sight of a police car being driven across the field towards them. It seemed to her that the strobing blue lights were aimed at her. She suddenly turned and strode towards the edge. Greg ran and leapt, grabbing her gilet. He landed with the gilet in his hands, but Joan was gone.

-o0o-

By the time DI Ian Harris arrived, the scene had changed dramatically. The sun was low on the horizon - the middle of 'the golden hour' as photographers call it.

Bob was sitting in the back of a police patrol car. Blue and white police tape encircled the caravan, and the cliff path was blocked in each direction. A crowd of campers stood around making conversation. An ambulance had arrived. The paramedics, having sat Greg down on the back step for a while to let him recover from the trauma, were waiting to see if they were needed any more. The Coast Guard Search and Rescue helicopter could be heard approaching in the distance.

The couple who had watched the exchange and the jump, though they couldn't hear everything that was said, had spoken to a police constable and been advised that they might be called as witnesses. Their witness statements would be taken at a later date.

DI Harris took his time speaking to Greg and Sally and finding out the circumstances that had led to the apparent suicide. He explained that Bob's part in 'aiding and abetting' the killer, his wife, and the likely charge of 'the prevention of the lawful and decent burial of a body' would be the responsibility of the Staffordshire Police Force.

It was just after half-past-nine when they were given leave to go home.

They shared the driving for the return journey. It wasn't the first time they had made this particular trip, but it was the most somber. It should have been a triumph to find the truth about what happened to Rebecca on that fateful evening. The triumph had been snatched away by the events of *this* tragic evening.

They considered calling Sharon, David and Robert, but decided that there had been enough drama for one day.

They weren't looking forward to the drive, but at that time on a Sunday night, the traffic was likely to be light. Nevertheless, they didn't expect to be home until one o'clock on Monday morning and they would have to get up for work as usual after they had managed to have some sleep.

Friday 14th September

43

St Philip's Church was packed for the memorial service of the late Rebecca Stainton. Sharon had not assumed she would lead the service, but David insisted that she should.

What she didn't expect was that Bishop Stephen, the Bishop of Stafford, an assistant bishop in the Lichfield Diocese, would turn up shortly before the service and ask her if she would like him to do anything. She knew it would be rude to say 'No', so she invited him to say a few words of introduction at the beginning, and The Blessing at the end.

At the front, as a focal point, there was a giant wine glass, nearly a metre high, filled with the pink bows. They had been collected together from all around the village and surrounding area. Some of the bows were more than four years old.

David sat on the front row with Robert, Mary, Joshua and Sarah Bailey. David and Robert both gave tributes to their wife and daughter respectively. They managed to mix humour with sadness, laughter with tears.

The service ended with one of Rebecca's favourite songs led by a choir of children from the school: *Lord of the Dance*. The joyful song left the congregation in a happy mood.

Refreshments were served in the Church Hall next door. It was an opportunity for people to speak to David more informally.

Not far away from him was a young lady with red hair, the colour of red wine. She had her son by her side. Sally noticed that she was wearing an engagement ring.

'Hello, Vanessa. Nice to see you again.'

'Hi Sally.'

'And this is your son?' she asked looking at the handsome young man.

'This is Nathan.' Then to Nathan, 'Say Hello, Nathan.'

'Hello.'

'That's probably all you're going to get out of him, I'm afraid. Well, he *is* seventeen.'

'How are things going?'

'With David? He's doing okay. He has his moments. Not surprising really.'

Sally leaned in close and whispered 'Congratulations' into her ear. Nothing else was said. It produced a big smile. Nathan wandered over to the food tables.

'It must be hard being a single mum of a teenager.'

'It is, but then I've been a single mum for a long time. I married young. It didn't last long. To be perfectly honest, I didn't really love him.'

'It must be hard for Nathan as well.'

'Sure.'

'Does he see his dad?'

'My ex hasn't been around since the divorce. He

remarried. Good luck to him.'

'So, nothing?'

'Nathan wouldn't know his father if he were in the same room.' Vanessa had something she was eager to tell Sally. 'You know the poem Rebecca wrote to David in her diary?'

'Yes.'

'I had it printed and it now sits in a frame on the top of the piano in his drawing room, next to the wedding photo of him and Rebecca. I know I can never replace her. They were so good together. Maybe one day he can learn to love me as much. That would make us both happy.'

'From what I've seen, I think you'll be good for him. Look, I'm glad I was able to speak to you and I really hope all goes well.' Sally looked around the room. 'Must go. I want to speak to some people over there. Bye.'

'Bye Sally. Stay safe.'

Sally worked her way through the crowd that had managed to squeeze into the Church Hall. She noticed a folded table tennis table pushed up against one wall and wondered if it were even possible to play a good game in such a small space. She picked up a cup of tea as she passed the kitchen hatch and greeted Denise, who was serving the drinks.

Doctor Jason Edwards and Gordon Pitcher, the manager of The Oaks, were standing together. 'Hello gentlemen. How are you?'

'Very well thank you,' replied Jason. Gordon nodded in agreement.

Sally lowered her voice so as not to be overheard by others around them. 'I've been meaning to ask, did anything happen in the wake of the suspicions about the deaths at The Oaks?'

'Ah that! I'm sure you'll be pleased to know that my colleagues at the Cambridge Road Practice scrutinised my conduct and found no evidence to pursue the matter. I think Rebecca was just *too* sensitive. Mind you, in the light of the Shipman Case, she was probably right to consider the possibility that something wasn't right.'

Gordon jumped in. 'We're quite satisfied that everything was done by the book and with complete transparency. It's just so sad that Rebecca was plagued by what she thought she was witnessing.'

'I'm very pleased for you,' she said.

'Thank you,' said Jason, bowing his head in acknowledgment.

Out of the corner of her eye she saw Greg coming through the door. It gave her a reason to make her excuses and move away from them.

'Where've you been?'

'I've been outside chatting to a few people. And you?'

'I've had a chat with Vanessa over there, and Jason and Gordon over there.' She indicated them with a nod of her head.

'And?'

'And all is good.'

'Well, I've just heard an amusing thing.'

'Yes...'

'Cliff, the guy who found the key to the crypt in the canal and then dragged up the bomb?'

'Yes....'

'He's given up magnet fishing. He's now into drone photography.'

'Goodness knows what he'll find next, then.'

'Just what I was thinking.'

'Shall we go now?'

'Let's just have a word with David, shall we?'

'Of course.'

David was standing with the four members of the Bailey family. Lots of people were wanting to speak to him. He spotted them and waved them closer. 'Greg. Sally. I'm pleased to see you. I want to say a really big thank you for taking up Sharon's challenge and solving the mystery of what happened to Rebecca. It wasn't what I most hoped and prayed for, but the truth is better than not knowing.'

'It was our pleasure,' said Greg proudly.

'I'm sure that you can now get on with your life. It's been 'on hold' a bit, hasn't it?'

'Exactly.'

Robert Bailey had been listening in. 'I'm looking forward to seeing David's smile again and hearing him joking as he did so often in the past.'

'The past has passed,' David commented, jovially.

'We better leave you to catch up with all these people.' Sally said firmly.

'Thank you again,' he said. 'Perhaps we'll meet again.'

'Perhaps.' They took leave of him and the Baileys and

headed for the door where Sharon and Simon were standing like sentinels.

'Glad you could come,' Sharon said. 'Please don't be strangers. You know where you can find me.'

'You haven't heard any more about Bob White, have you?' asked Greg.

'Not much. I do know he's on conditional bail staying with his sister in Stoke.'

'I guess, like us, you've been told not to speak to him in case we're called as witnesses.'

'Yes. But I've heard on the grapevine that his case is due to be held before the end of the year and that he intends to plead guilty to concealing Rebecca's body.'

'Any idea what that will mean for him.'

'Again, I don't really know, though I'm led to believe that he'll probably be given a custodial sentence of perhaps two years - less if he's lucky.'

Sally was thoughtful. 'He must be in a terrible state with all that hanging over him and dealing with the loss of Joan.'

'And being cut off from St Saviour's. The church has been a major part of his life for so long.'

'We'll just have to wait and see, won't we?'

Sharon changed the subject. 'You met Jack Taylor, didn't you?'

'We did.' said Sally. 'We visited him at his home back in June to tell him what happened - all about finding Rebecca, and finding Bob and Joan in Chetmouth.'

'I heard earlier,' Sharon said solemnly, 'that he died

peacefully at home this morning. He'd have loved to have been here.'

'I'm sure he would. That's really sad. He thought a lot of her, didn't he?'

'For sure.'

They shared a somber moment until Sally changed the subject. 'Just one thing,' insisted Sally, 'if you have any more mysteries to solve, ask someone else. Okay?'

'Okay.' Simon and Sharon laughed together.

-o0o-

Greg and Sally were sitting up in bed reading. Sally was distracted by the events and conversations of the evening. 'Did I tell you?' she said, and waited until Greg finished the paragraph of his Lee Child's book and could give her his full attention.

'Tell me what?'

'That I had a chat with Vanessa and met her son. His name's Nathan.'

'That's a name from the Bible, isn't it?'

'I think so.'

Greg grabbed his mobile and Googled *Nathan in the Bible*. 'Yes,' he said. 'He was one of King David's sons.'

'Ohhh' said Sally knowingly. 'Now that *is* interesting.'

Greg looked at her quizzically.

'Never mind, dear. You don't need to know.' *I wonder if he knows.*

The Author

Paul Knight was brought up in a village near Burton-on-Trent in Staffordshire. He left school to work in retail. After a move to Swanage in Dorset, he was employed as a Civil Servant working with MOD (Army) at Bovington Camp.

From there, he trained as a minister in the Church of England. He served in various places around the country before being appointed as Vicar of a parish in West Yorkshire where he stayed for twenty-three years.

Married to Annette, they have three children, six grandchildren and two dogs.

Now retired, they live in the Rhondda Valley in Wales, in Annette's childhood home.

Paul discovered writing as a hobby and a holiday pastime. His writing has been described as a cross between Dan Brown and Enid Blyton! His response: *I'll take it as a compliment to be compared with either.*

Have you read these books in the series?

Fifteen Elizabeth Avenue
Jackie has been living at 15 Elizabeth Avenue with Steve for three years when she discovers something in the loft which makes her suspicious about the last occupant.
Now she fears for her life and asks Greg, an old friend, for help. Will he, can he, save her?

Run Boy. Run!
A short stay for Greg and Sally Williams at a Holiday Centre in the Welsh mountains turns into a hunt when Sally goes missing. Cryptic messages and puzzles lead on a dangerous chase which may end in a happy reunion or capture with fatal consequences.

A Tragic Accident
One of the members of Greg and Sally's pub quiz team falls to his death from the Cornish Coastal Path. Not all is at it seems.
A coded letter is expected to reveal what really happened. Yet more dangers lie ahead for the quiz team and more lives are at stake.

Sky High Revenge
A holiday in the Caribbean turns out to be less than relaxing. It becomes clear that there are motives for resentment among their fellow guests, but how far will someone go to wreak revenge. With time running out, it's up to Greg and Sally to work it all out.

A Stroke of Bad Luck
Blakeley's Golf Club becomes the centre of attention when it hosts a Charity Celebrity Pro-Am Tournament. The success of the day is wrecked by those looking for personal gain. Greg and Sally work with the police to discover the facts and bring about justice.

All available from ghbooks.uk